He stepped closer and brushed a stray curl off her cheek.

"Asher..." Longing flickered across her face. Maggie bit her lower lip.

"Yeah?"

"You're flirting with me." She said it softly, warily, as if she couldn't decide if she liked it or not.

"Yeah."

Her brow furrowed. "And you're at work."

"Is that the only reason you don't like it?"

As if by habit, she rested a hand on the dog's back. Jackson sent Asher a dubious look.

I know, buddy. Crashing hard, here.

Her chest rose with a deep breath. Her earlier flush returned to her cheeks. "Who said I didn't like it?"

"A hunch."

She glanced over her shoulder and around him before rising up to steal a kiss.

* * *

SUTTER CREEK, MONTANA:
Passion and happily-ever-afters in Big Sky Country

Dear Reader,

Characters often come to me fully formed, and Asher Matsuda is an example of that. The bisexual widower had a cameo in his brother Caleb's book, *Holiday by Candlelight*. Given the advice he shared with Caleb, I knew Asher still believed in love, even after losing his husband to cancer. I had a sexy-as-all-get-out mental picture of a brawny bearded man shelving books and leading children's story time. I also knew he was a loving father who was willing to make a life-altering change—moving across the country—because he believed he and his daughter, Ruth, needed a new start.

Asher trusts his second chance at love will show up at the right time, for him and Ruth. Local veterinarian Maggie Reid doesn't believe there's ever a right time for that kind of vulnerability, but when the dog she's training bonds with Asher and Ruth, she can't help but wonder if the canine is onto something. There's something irresistible about the kind-hearted librarian. Especially when he's wielding a hammer in an attempt to make some extra cash to facilitate Ruth's ski-racing team fees. The newcomers have Maggie questioning long-held beliefs. Does she have room for romance and motherhood—and a giant goofy dog—in her life after all?

I'd love to hear your own goofy-dog stories. Come find me on Facebook, Instagram and Pinterest (laurelgreerauthor) to share your best canine adventures.

Happy reading,

Laurel

In Service of Love

LAUREL GREER

HARLEQUIN
SPECIAL
EDITION

HARLEQUIN®

SPECIAL EDITION™

Recycling programs
for this product may
not exist in your area.

ISBN-13: 978-1-335-89480-9

In Service of Love

Copyright © 2020 by Lindsay Macgowan

This edition published by arrangement with Harlequin Books S.A.

For questions and comments about the quality of this book, please contact us at CustomerService@Harlequin.com.

Harlequin Enterprises ULC
22 Adelaide St. West, 40th Floor
Toronto, Ontario M5H 4E3, Canada
www.Harlequin.com

Printed in U.S.A.

Raised in a small town on Vancouver Island, **Laurel Greer** grew up skiing and boating by day and reading romances under the covers by flashlight at night. Ever committed to the proper placement of the Canadian *eh*, she loves to write books with snapping sexual tension and second chances. She lives outside Vancouver with her law-talking husband and two daughters. At least half her diet is made up of tea. Find her at www.laurelgreer.com.

Books by Laurel Greer

Harlequin Special Edition

Sutter Creek, Montana

From Exes to Expecting
A Father for Her Child
Holiday by Candlelight
Their Nine-Month Surprise

Chapter One

Is that dog reading?

Asher Matsuda did a double take before polishing the lenses of his glasses. Ignoring the mess of returned books in the library's intake bin, he mentally scribbled "literate canine" on his overflowing never-thought-I'd-see-that list.

A Great Dane, its short coat almost cadet blue in color, stared intently at the shelf of books in front of him. The dog had to outweigh his handler by half. The petite blonde woman wore scrubs. One of her pale hands rested on the service vest between the dog's shoulder blades. She dragged a finger of the other along the spines of the true crime section.

Huh. Her no-nonsense, curly bob and the serious tilt to her rosy mouth gave off the impression of a memoir reader, probably of political science or history-focused books.

But if anyone knew not to put people in boxes, it was a bisexual, male librarian with a penchant for reading romance novels and blowing out electric guitar amps. And if Asher had a dollar for every time he'd been told he'd look more at home on a football field than behind a circulation desk, he'd have enough money to fund his ten-year-old daughter's dream of being a Supreme Court Justice. When Asher and his late husband had named her after one of their modern-day heroes, Ruth Bader Ginsburg, they hadn't anticipated Ruth would follow her namesake's example so damn literally.

He sneaked another peek at the towering, lanky dog and its handler, who had moved one row over into the nonfiction section. The Great Dane was now perusing the selection of WWII books as the woman played eeny meeny miney moe on the shelf above. Right around the Dewey decimal range for nineteenth-century Europe. *Ha!* His earlier prediction hadn't been totally off base.

She glanced his way, catching his gaze and fixing him with a look.

Something along the lines of: *stop staring, weirdo.*

He sent her an apologetic smile and ducked behind the desk to pull out the wheeled book return bin. The last thing he could afford was to be known as the creepy new guy. He and Ruth had moved to town a little under a month ago, not long enough for people to have gotten to know them yet. Sutter Creek seemed inviting, and his older brother, who'd moved here himself a year ago, would never have suggested Asher follow suit had he not believed it to be safe. But Asher had been out long enough that he knew the moment people realized he was bi, not gay, it often meant an even harder road to acceptance.

He busied himself dealing with the minutiae of library work: checking books back in, processing patron requests, processing new arrivals. Shifting from a larger branch in Brooklyn to Sutter Creek, Montana's tiny outpost, with its two-person staff, was no minor change, and he was still getting accustomed to the slower speed of small-town life. But his new position was an opportunity to essentially run a branch, a promotion that would have taken him another decade to move into in New York. He'd needed the challenge, and the raise, after being widowed.

The front doors opened and his daughter bounced in, wiping her feet on the mat. A gust of early October wind ruffled the posters pinned to the tackboard lining the wall across from the circulation desk. He'd had plenty of time to read the advertisements for community trivia night and Wing Wednesday at one of the local pubs, but hadn't managed to explore any social options yet. Maybe now that Ruth was a month into the school year, he could look for a group of people interested in a regular jam session or a book club. He and Ruth had been welcomed warmly at the synagogue they'd started attending in Bozeman, but services were only held every second Saturday, and it was a bit of a drive. Better to make friends locally as quickly as he could, and ensure Ruth did the same.

She waved, rushing forward. "Dad, guess what!"

A canine yelp sounded from the other side of the library, between the shelves. Asher jerked his gaze from his approaching daughter to the dog, who was cowering at his person's side. The corners of the woman's mouth turned down and her shoulders slumped momentarily, before she straightened and motioned to the dog with an upturned hand.

"Library voice, love," he reminded Ruth. They had a good routine going. The elementary school was only a few blocks from the library, so she came to the branch after the last bell and did homework or read until closing time. Saved a hell of a lot on after-school care costs and let him keep an eye on her, too.

She dropped her backpack on the floor and draped herself across the waist-high counter. Her feet swung, and the toes of her sneakers thunked dully on the front of the desk.

The dog whined again, and Asher winced. But he couldn't bring himself to go full taskmaster-librarian on her. When was the last time Ruth had bounded toward him like she had just now? Before

Alex's terminal diagnosis almost two years ago? He smiled encouragingly. "Remember, quiet body, too."

"Sorry, Dad."

He shuffled his armful of paperbacks onto the counter and tugged on his daughter's windblown, dark brown ponytail. People got confused as to how Ruth had Asher's Japanese grandfather's stick-straight hair and Alex's bright smile. One of the easier questions he got about his family. Science, and the generosity of Alex's cousin, who'd been their egg donor and surrogate.

He couldn't be more thankful that Ruth had ended up with that particular dimpled grin. And it was dialed up to full wattage this afternoon.

"That looks like the face of a girl who's happy with the topic of her science inquiry project."

Her grin widened, *future expensive orthodontic bills* written all over her adorably crooked front teeth. "I am! It's going to be epic."

Oh man. She was solidly in tween mode, and her moments of sounding older than she was never failed to amuse him. "Black holes?"

She shook her head. *"Skiing."*

He blinked at her in puzzlement and adjusted the cuffs of his dress shirt. "Say what, now? Wouldn't that be for gym class?"

"No, Dad. The physics of it. Racing. Did you know Olympians ski between 75 and 95 miles an hour?"

He did. He also knew that avalanches moved at about the same speed, and ever since his older brother, Caleb, had been caught in one, racing down a slope had lost its shine. But then, without that avalanche, Caleb would still be in Denver, lonely and hurting. The charming Montana ski town—and the wonderful woman Caleb had fallen in love with—had provided a safe space to heal. Asher was hoping Sutter Creek would be the same for Ruth and him. The uncertainty of moving was a thousand times better than watching Ruth stare at the wall of her bedroom in the basement in his parents' Brooklyn brownstone with tears on her apple-round cheeks.

"I get bonus marks if I can test my hypothesis," she said.

"Hypothesis, huh? You sound like Papa." Alex had been a high school science teacher. Damn good one, too. Ruth had been spouting four-syllable words since preschool.

Her smile wobbled. "Can I take ski lessons? Harper and Fallon said there's a team. With competitions and everything."

"Bit early in the season for that, honey." He mentally added the cost of equipment rentals, passes and lessons to the ongoing tally of future orthodontia and college. *Ouch.* Even with his raise, going from two incomes down to one meant a strained budget. "The mountain doesn't open for a couple of months."

Her toes collided with the desk again, and an animal whine sounded from over near the magazines. Weren't assistance dogs supposed to be silent unless they were alerting to something? The cute blonde owner seemed to have her hands full.

As did he, with almost five feet of precocious ten-year-old.

"I *know*," Ruth insisted. "But my teacher says I can hand in that part later."

Maybe his brother's fiancée, who patrolled for the mountain, would be able to apply her employee discount to Ruth's costs. Learning to ski might be affordable, but joining a racing team would be astronomical. "We'll see, okay?"

Ruth narrowed her hazel eyes. "That means no."

No, that meant moving across the country had dug way too far into what remained of Alex's life insurance after paying funeral home and hospital co-pay bills. But Asher wasn't going to lay that on his daughter's shoulders. He knew how to stretch his salary. He also needed to make sure he wasn't quashing her attempts to make friends, and she'd dropped the names Harper and Fallon a few times this week.

"Skiing is a big commitment, Ruthie. Why don't we go to the community center this weekend, see if there's an activity a little less involved? Dance, or floor hockey."

She slid off the counter and crossed her arms over her teal fleece jacket. "You don't feel like you're flying when you do *ballet*, Dad."

"You might. Grand jetés are pretty impressive."

She rolled her eyes. "A ballerina would go max—" she stared into space for a second, lips moving silently "—4 miles an hour. That's at least 70 miles slower. Not fast enough."

He shook his head. The kid had never met a fact she didn't love, and her inner calculator was mind-boggling at times. But the speed demon desire was new. "We'll *see*."

"Whatever." She snatched her backpack off the ground and stomped around the desk toward the staff office behind him. "I have *homework*."

She slammed the door.

The Dane howled, a mournful peal.

"Easy, Jacks." The woman emerged from behind a shelf with the dog on a short lead, tail between his legs. Her eyes sparked with irritation.

"I'm sorry about the noise," Asher mumbled. "I—"

But before he could finish his apology, the woman froze in her tracks. The dog nudged her ankle with his nose, and a click sounded. She took one step forward, then cried out and crumpled to the floor.

Maggie Reid lay on the floor for a few seconds, mimicking the periodic collapses of a person with Parkinson's. The Dane was nearing the end of his training, but for his itty-bitty issue with sudden noises. Good gravy. If being at a library startled the gentle giant, she had no hope of acclimatizing him to street noise.

She sighed and rose on her elbows. At least in standing still at her side, waiting for her to use his harness to help her get off the floor, Jackson was following protocol—

"Can I help you?" A rich baritone, rent with concern, interrupted her attempt to train her charge. "I don't want to interfere if you have everything under control, but you went down pretty hard, and—"

"I'm pretending," she cut in.

The librarian came to a halt a few feet away from her. His almost-black brows drew together, making his glasses slide down a bit. He shoved up the thick-rimmed, navy-colored frames and rubbed his fingers along his bearded cheek. From her semiprone position, he towered over her like a freaking pine tree. Wowza. Her friend Garnet had not lied when she'd described her brother-in-law-to-be as an academic mountain man.

"Pretending?" he repeated, a faint New York accent bending the syllables. He crouched beside her. His dark jeans stretched across muscular thighs, cuffed once, showing off some really pretty brown Chelsea boots. A hint of sage drifted to her nose.

She held in an appreciative sigh. "I'm training Jackson here to be a service dog."

The wrinkles of concern relaxed around his brown eyes. "Ah. I didn't realize."

She winced. "Of course, you didn't. I've been training dogs for years, and most everyone in town is used to me affecting various physical needs during sessions. I should have warned you. I'm sorry."

She grabbed the dog's harness and mimicked the deliberate motions of a person with neurodegenerative symptoms. Once on her feet, she used the clicker to let the dog know he'd correctly completed his task, then lavished him with whispers of "good boy" and ear scratches. After nuzzling the sweet beast once more for good measure, she stuck out her hand to the librarian, who had stood while she praised the dog. "Maggie Reid."

"Asher Matsuda," he said, holding the books she'd dropped when she'd hit the ground. "But knowing Sutter Creek, that's probably old information." He took her hand in his large, warm grip. She shivered. A woman could find uses for hands like those.

"I did know your name, but because of Garnet, not town gossip," she said. Well, because of Asher's almost-sister-in-law *and* town gossip, to be specific.

"You know Garnet?"

"Yep. I'm on the search and rescue crew with her."

"Dogs, veterinary medicine, search and rescue and—" he glanced at the instruction manuals in his hand "—cabinetry and flooring. You're a woman of many talents."

And a busy one. The hour she'd cleared out of her appointment schedule to work with Jackson on running errands was almost up. She glanced at the clock over the circulation desk where, a few minutes ago, she'd been trying not to stare at Asher as he'd joked around with his daughter. Up until the slamming door, that was. But that was preteens for you. "My brother's building a dog training facility onto the back of my clinic, and we're trying to do some of the interior finishing ourselves."

His slow-spreading smile sent tingles skittering through her limbs. "If you have any questions, ask. I used to work construction back when I was young and naive and playing guitar didn't pay the bills."

Maggie bit her lip. Strap a tool belt around his waist and dirty up those jeans a bit, and yeah, she could see him wielding a hammer. She could picture him with an electric guitar slung around his broad shoulders, too. His stacked leather-and-metal bracelets would clink against the body of the instrument, cradled below his flat abs... *Mmm.* No. That full, groomed beard and wavy hair had to belong to an acoustic player. Ballads in a coffee shop for this guy.

Mouth suddenly dry, she swallowed. "The glamor of library science won out?"

He laughed. "That, and parenting."

Oof, those glasses were sexy. As was a man who embraced his responsibility.

Had her dad ever talked about being a father in such an affectionate manner?

Don't even go there, Maggie. Dating anyone, let

alone a single parent, was a big no-no in her books—
why start something up that would inevitably end
and scar a poor kid in the process? But had she been
looking for something serious, Asher Matsuda would
have been an interesting candidate.

Provided he was interested in women, too. Garnet had mentioned he'd lost his husband last year.

"I should, uh, run those books through the self-
checkout," she said. "Jacks and I have to get back
to work."

He put a hand to the placket of his button-down.
Her brain so wanted to read that as a *hey, Maggie,
look at my pecs* signal. She flicked her gaze upward
before she could properly evaluate the state of his
chest. Wasn't fair to check someone out who didn't
necessarily welcome the attention.

"You'll put me out of a job," he teased, turning on
a boot heel and taking her books behind the circulation desk. He raised a brow as Jackson ambled up beside her, nose reaching the top of the counter. "Your
buddy there could probably even bowl me over."

She shook her head. "He's well trained."

"Minus the yelping?"

With a humph, she narrowed her eyes. "He's just
easily startled."

Doubt crossed his face. "I—"

She slapped her library card down on the counter.
The dog whimpered.

Jitters spread in Maggie's stomach. Yeah, two-thirds of dogs failed their service training. But of the six dogs she had trained to date for an organization in Missoula, she had a perfect record. There wasn't any official licensing process, but between Maggie and Lachlan, they had a spotless reputation, Lachlan with search and rescue dogs, Maggie with service animals. And once her brother's expansion was up and running, he'd hire more staff and have a larger capacity.

"Seems you have your hands full with that guy," Asher finished quietly, passing over the checked-out instruction manuals. Their hands brushed, sending a shimmer of warmth up her arm. Her breath caught and she glanced at his face to make sure he hadn't picked up on the reaction.

His brown eyes were a little wide behind those sexy nerd glasses. *Agh*, he *had* noticed, and was no doubt trying to figure out how to let her down gently. He probably had to fend off admirers on an hourly basis. He had no way of knowing she would never count herself among them.

"Uh, Dad?" A small voice with an East Coast inflection equal to Asher's came from over his shoulder. "I need help with— Ooh, that dog is so pretty. He's *blue*."

The girl had the awkward look of a kid who'd grown a whole lot in a short period of time. She was almost as tall as Maggie, not that five feet one was a height to aspire to. The girl rushed to her dad's side. When her gaze fell on Jackson's vest, her smile faded. "Oh. He's working."

Maggie nodded. "Thanks for noticing. It's important not to pet him."

"I know. One of my friends at my old Hebrew school had a dog to help him with his autism." She bit her lip before adding hopefully, "But sometimes, I would visit his apartment and the dog got to take off his vest so I could pet him…"

"Ruthie," Asher warned quietly.

"It's okay," Maggie said, unable to resist the hope in his daughter's expression. "Maybe after Jackson finishes his training."

If Jackson finishes his training.

The faint chime of the Episcopalian church bell marking the hour filtered through the closed front door. She grimaced. "Crud, I'm late. See you around."

"I look forward to it." A hint of pleasure tilted one corner of Asher's mouth up. Good, she hadn't crossed any lines too badly… It spread to a full-on curious smile as he continued with, "Books are due in two weeks."

So was Jackson—in two weeks, Maggie's brother would formally assess the Dane for suitability as a service dog.

Could she get this done in time while managing her clinic and following through on her promises to help her brother with his construction work? Anxious pressure built in her chest. Muttering her thanks and returning Asher's casual wave, she led the dog out of the library, groaning as he cowered at the thud, thud, thud of approaching skateboard wheels on the wooden, raised sidewalk.

She raised her palm to bring him to attention. *Come on, big guy. You gotta figure this out.*

For his own sake, and hers.

The only thing Maggie disliked more than relationships was failure.

Chapter Two

"Dad, I told you, I don't want to sign up for floor hockey!"

Asher sucked in a calming breath as his daughter's voice careened toward a whine. Three days had passed since he suggested she try something other than skiing, and he was no closer to convincing her. "I'm not saying you have to. But you should give something a try."

They sat in the atrium of the Sutter Mountain Community Center. The registration desk ran one side of the airy, glass-fronted space, and a few people stood in line, waiting to pay to get in for the Sunday morning public swim. The entrance to the pool sat kitty-corner to a small coffee bar. Asher and Ruth occupied one of the tables, the remnants of their lunch gathered in red plastic sandwich baskets.

He shoved the magazine-sized registration guide toward his daughter. "Here. If you're not liking what I'm suggesting, then show me what looks good."

She riffled to the back of the guide, smacked the page open and pushed it back to him. "Harper said training and fundraising have already started!"

A glossy advertisement splashed across the inside cover, the kids in the assortment of pictures either laughing in their snow gear or racing pell-mell down a hill.

His heart sank.

"Ruth." He slid off his glasses and massaged the tight muscles around his eyes. "What about just taking lessons from Garnet and Uncle Caleb this season? And then if you really like it, we can see about racing next winter." That would give him more time to squirrel away money for club fees and expensive equipment.

"But I want to race *now*."

"Your enthusiasm is admirable, peanut, but I'm not sure joining the club is in the cards this year."

Her mouth tightened at the corners. "Da-*ad*."

Full-on whine-zone. Ten-year-old achievement: unlocked. He resisted the urge to pull out the, "I can't understand you when you're whining," strategy he and Alex had used during Ruth's preschool and kindergarten years. He put his glasses back on. "Try again, Ruthie."

Her throat bobbed. "You never said no to me trying new things back home."

Ouch. That one landed right between the ribs. Her voice had dropped to little-girl small. He hated anything that stole her spark. Especially when he was the thief.

"I thought we agreed not to compare Sutter Creek and New York," he said.

She crossed her arms over the sequin star spangling the front of her T-shirt. Her lip wobbled and her gaze darted to the side. She didn't answer.

"It's normal to do that, though," he said. "I miss Brooklyn, too."

And Alex.

Though when Maggie had been in the library, her eyes had locked on his, and he'd felt about thirty pounds lighter. For a second, he'd wondered if there was room for something new in his life. Someone.

Ruth screwed her face up. Tears glinted on her lashes.

Ah, hell. What was he thinking? Sutter Creek might be *their* new beginning, but it wasn't *his* new beginning. It was still too soon. For his sake, and for Ruth's.

"I'm not sad because of moving." She directed her claim toward the coffee counter, not to him, an obvious tell she wasn't being honest. "I'm mad because you won't let me ski."

And because I moved you across the country.

And cancer stole your Papa.

Stole my love.

Reality struck. They'd lost all that, and he wasn't doing what he could to give her something healthy she was asking for? Rubbing the heel of his hand across his forehead, he scrambled for a compromise. Maybe Garnet knew the club operators and could swing a discount for him. Or was there a way he could make some extra cash to refill the incidentals budget? His hours at work were fixed, so there weren't any extra shifts at the branch. Maybe one of the local bars had a slot for a solo musician that would pay something? He snorted at the prospect. He hadn't performed in years, unless singing along to Lady Gaga in the car with Ruth counted.

"I'll see what I can do, okay?" he said.

Ruth wasn't paying attention. She straightened in her chair, staring raptly at the giant blue-gray dog leading his handler past the pool entrance and toward the seating area where Asher and Ruth were sitting. "It's that same dog!"

"So it is." Who could pay attention to the furry monster when his lead was being held by Maggie Reid, though? Asher's heart skipped a beat. *Wow.* A year ago, he'd thought his heart would never start beating again, let alone react to someone who wasn't the man he'd loved since he was nineteen.

Maggie wore a long-sleeved T-shirt, a flirty skirt and patterned leggings. A human rainbow, nothing like the plain scrubs she'd had on when she came into the library. A wrap headband held her halo of blond curls off her face. Intense curiosity rose in his belly—her hair looked like it might be soft, but who knew with curls? Alex's had been coarse to the point that he'd never let his hair grow out longer than half an inch. But Maggie's—her locks bounced, and they were kinda loose. Maybe they—

"Dad, you're staring."

He jolted. "I am?"

Ruth's brow knit. "Why are you smiling like that?"

Ah, crap. "Like what?"

"Like… I don't know. It's weird." Ruth rolled her eyes before waving at Maggie. "Hi, Dr. Reid!"

Maggie startled, jumping almost as much as the dog did on his short lead. She lifted a hand in greeting.

"Ruth," Asher growled.

"What? I used my manners," she defended.

"That you did." He lifted one corner of his mouth up, trying to wordlessly apologize to Maggie for Ruth having caught her off guard.

Maggie nodded back and kept going, then seemed to question her decision, veering toward them instead of continuing on to the coffee counter. She stopped a few feet from their table, as did the Dane. The canine was so tall he lined up eye to eye with Asher, seated in his chair.

"Maggie Reid," Asher greeted. "And the fearless wonder dog."

She grimaced. "I wish. I'm going to have to get pretty intensive with this guy. He hid from the neighborhood flock of starlings this morning."

"I want to play with him so badly," Ruth said hopefully. "But I know what you said about him working."

Maggie pursed her lips in contemplation. "There's a dog park around back of the pool. If you aren't busy, you could come with me. I'd like to see him around kids when he isn't in uniform."

Ruth perked up.

"Once Ruth here picks an activity to sign up for, we could come for a bit," Asher suggested.

Ruth's smile faded. "Nothing looks good."

Nothing that didn't cost a fortune.

"Do you like chill activities, Ruth, or stuff that's more exciting?" the veterinarian asked.

"Definitely exciting," Ruth said. "My friends are on the ski racing team, and I want to join, too."

Maggie shifted her gaze to Asher, lips parted as if she was holding back a question.

He gave her a little headshake, guilt squeezing

his insides over not being able to fill his daughter's request.

"There's swimming, too," Maggie suggested. "And I know it doesn't involve speed at all, but the artist who teaches afternoon classes in the multipurpose room is mega talented."

"I don't know." Ruth's mouth pressed in a stubborn line. It was like looking at his mom when Ruth made that face. And just like her, Ruth didn't respond well to bulldozing. Plus, he didn't want to provoke a blowup in front of a virtual stranger. "Tell you what, Ruth. Why don't we go to the dog park first? Maybe some fresh air will help you decide. We can sign you up for something after."

She acquiesced with a wary nod.

"Lead the way," he said, motioning to Maggie. He hadn't pictured Sunday including time with a cute veterinarian, but he couldn't say he minded. Even if his appreciation was going to have to stay hands-off.

He followed Maggie and her furry shadow out a glass door. Her tennis-style skirt twitched as she walked. Something in his chest twitched in response.

Don't get carried away there, champ.

The path was wide enough for two plus a dog, and wound past a grassy patch and a row of pine trees. It ended at a fenced enclosure where a Lab and a Jack Russell were playing fetch with their owner. He jogged a couple of steps to catch up to Maggie.

"You know," he said conversationally, "my twin is a vet."

"You have a twin?" She ran her teeth along her lower lip. Her gaze was fixed somewhere on his chest or arms. Good move on hitting the free weights he kept in his garage before heading out this morning. "Are you, uh, identical?"

He shook his head. "Fraternal. And Dave takes after my mom's side of the family. He's all Klein." The past rushed in and he snorted. "Teachers had a hard time believing my brothers and I were related, given Caleb looks more like our dad and I resemble both sides."

"I got that with my older sister sometimes— we don't look alike aside from our hair color." She winced. "It's not the same, is it?"

"Not entirely. But you should hear some of the questions I get about Ruth having two fathers. Being biracial is nothing in comparison." He paused, unsure of how much to divulge. Maggie seemed accepting so far, and admitting a few of his worries to her might give him a read on how many problems he could anticipate facing. "It was one of my biggest fears about moving—how people in a new town would accept me. Ruth, too."

Her lips twisted thoughtfully. "I would hope Sutter Creek proves your fears unfounded, but I know that's naïve. My receptionist is gay, and he and his boyfriend talk about microaggressions now and then. No major safety issues, to my knowledge." She glanced at his daughter, who had skipped past them and was waiting by the gate to the off-leash area. "You're a good dad."

He cocked a brow. "How do you know? You've spent all of twenty minutes with us."

Her contemplative smile flattened, as if some kind of intrinsic awareness was weighing down the corners. "I can tell."

A twinge of curiosity ran up his neck. "My twin is like that. Reads people like he does animals." Which—that wasn't what she was doing. She wasn't using animal sense; she was talking from personal experience. He pointed at the dog. "You sure seem to understand this guy."

"Not as well as I'd like. He's got me a bit puzzled."

She opened the gate and waited for Asher and Ruth to go through before following with Jackson.

He leaned toward his daughter. "Make sure to follow Maggie's lead, okay?" A dog that big could knock over an unaware kid. Hell, an unaware grownup, even.

"I will," she promised. "What should I do, Dr. Reid?"

Maggie unclipped the dog from the short lead and removed his vest. "Just play with him. He's off duty."

Ruth half crouched with her hands on her knees. "Jackson, wanna run?" she said in a goofy tone.

The dog cocked his head and bowed back, his tail sticking up in the air like a question mark.

"Let's go!" Ruth took off.

Jackson followed, springing forward as if he'd been launched from a trebuchet.

Asher chucked at the gangly frolicking. "Graceful, that one."

"A breed trait, for sure," Maggie joked.

When he grinned, a hint of interest lit her eyes. Just for a second. She seemed to check herself, and that inner flash of light dimmed.

"So why dog training?" he asked. Pried, really. But why not? She intrigued him. All sorts of layers wrapped in one petite package.

"Why library science?" she volleyed back. She wore her question like a protective veil.

She might not want to dish up answers, but he had nothing to hide. "I get to help people root out solutions. Nothing's more important than knowledge."

Her brow furrowed. "Nothing?"

"Money, possessions, love—nothing permanent there. But you carry your wits and experience with you, no matter what."

"Such a realist. I'd have pegged you as a romantic for some reason. But maybe losing your…" She shut her eyes in regret as she trailed off. "Sorry."

"It's okay." He didn't mind her openness. Didn't mind being open in return, even though it meant digging into the tender parts of his heart. "I can talk about it. Losing Alex was more painful than I'd ever guessed possible," he said, throat tight, words strained. "But I'd never sacrifice the time we did have together, no matter how much it felt like my soul was ripping in two to watch him fade away. And if I'm lucky enough, I'll find another equally fantastic partner at some point, when Ruth is ready. And have some more awesome years to make the hard parts worthwhile."

"An equally fantastic…man?" she asked, cheeks red. She immediately cringed. "*Ugh*. Don't answer that. You don't have to explain who and what floats your boat to some random—"

He waved a hand. But after gaining silence, he wasn't sure how he wanted to fill it. He'd known moving to a new town would mean coming out more than once. He'd run into situations where it was easier or safer to just let people believe he was gay because of his marriage to Alex. Being attracted to more than one gender meant living between two worlds at times. But Maggie had at least recognized he might also be attracted to more than just men. Somewhat of a semi win, though his stomach twisted nonetheless. "Women, too."

She nodded before replying. "Thanks for telling me. You didn't owe me that."

He took a deep breath. "Sometimes it can complicate things. Bisexuality gets misunderstood. But people will eventually find out, so it's a matter of picking my messengers and hoping my neighbor still waves at me when he comes in from his morning run. And if he doesn't, well, then I know."

"I hope he does." Her mouth tilted as she mulled something over. "I'm impressed you're open to finding someone new after being widowed… That's brave. I don't think I could…"

He waited a few seconds for her to finish. When she didn't, he said, "Sure you could. Anyone can be brave after a loss."

Resiliency had been one of the things that had drawn Asher to Alex. Asher's husband had created a found family after his parents had denounced his sexuality and cut him out of their lives. Alex had insisted on deserving and finding love, and had built an incredible, albeit too short, life with Asher and Ruth and all sorts of friends and extended family. Asher, too, had tried his best to overcome the prejudicial baggage others dumped on him. There was no other way to embrace all life had to offer. So to see Maggie hold back from possibilities hurt his heart.

"Being careful matters, too." She broke away from his gaze, staring across the pen at Ruth and Jackson playing a makeshift game of fetch.

A shadow crossed her face, like a cloud blown in front of the sun. It reminded him of his brother after the avalanche. What avalanche had swept up Maggie, tumbled and shaken and buried her?

He wanted to find out, to explore all of her dark

corners and hidden angles. But given how she'd shut down his question about why she trained service animals, he wasn't about to probe further.

Silence stretched, a minute of way too much awkwardness. He may have just spilled his life's philosophy to this woman, but they barely knew each other. If he had to guess, he'd venture that not many people at all knew Maggie Reid.

Would she let him?

And I'm so intent on this because...?

A horn honked from the nearby street. Jackson yelped and tried to hide behind Ruth.

"Crumbs," Maggie muttered, then called for the dog.

Ruth followed, concern on her face. "Did I do something wrong?"

"No, he's just scared." Maggie crouched down and stroked the dog. "He's afraid of sudden noises."

"You going to be able to fix that?" Asher said.

"I honestly don't know." She looked like she was trying to slide behind the same closed-off shield she'd worn a few minutes ago, but it wasn't staying in place. Her mouth turned down at the corners, and she buried her face in the dog's neck. After a few seconds, she pulled away and straightened. "My brother's fiancée is working on her doctorate in canine psychology and has been giving me advice, but it's not an easy process. I need more time to desensitize him. And my stupid promise to help Lachlan with the inside of his training facility is complicating that."

"Hence the books on interior finishing you checked out from the library," he said.

"Yeah. We initially planned on doing it ourselves to save money. But Lachlan's in the throes of being a new dad, and I've got this beast to shape up." She smiled at Ruth, who was waiting, mouth screwed up, clearly unsure as to whether she could still play with the dog. "Go on, Jacks. Go run."

Ruth's face relaxed and she bounded off, the dog at her heels.

"And you're feeling like you overcommitted?" he asked. "I get that. Ruth wants to join the ski racing club, and I don't know how I'm going to make that happen. It's expensive. But I want to. I want her to be happy, to consider Sutter Creek home."

Maggie nodded. "It's hard to move to a small town. This was never home for me, not entirely. My brother and I lived here during the summers, but we were at boarding school during the school year, unlike our older half-sister, who lived here year-round. I was always jealous of Stella's roots."

"And your parents were here?"

The wind stirred, blowing the curls around her face. She pushed them back with a hand and shook her head. "They were—are—in Chicago. We lived with our grandparents during our summer holidays.

And then I bought out the clinic from my grandfather when he was ready to retire."

He should have been happy with that offering. She was sharing personal information, after all. But it was…surface. He could have found out more from chatting up the friendly woman who owned the bakery near the library. "And now you're expanding."

"Sort of. Not my part of the business—I'm full up. But my brother has wanted to build a search and rescue dog school since he caught the SAR bug in high school. He's close. The bones and siding of the barn are renovated, and now we need to deal with the interior." She sighed. "Even if we wanted to hire someone, which we honestly would consider at this point, the contractors in town are booked solid for months."

The accountant in his brain clapped with joy. Hello, incidentals-budget supplement. "I'm not."

She narrowed her eyes. "What do you mean?"

"I know how to do interior finishing. And I'd be cheaper than hiring a professional carpenter."

"Oh. That's…" Consideration played across her pretty face. "You'd have time for that?"

"I'd make time. Friday nights and Saturdays are earmarked for family stuff and often Shabbat, but I could do other evenings and Sundays. As long as it would be okay to bring Ruth with me." Not the most exciting outing for a kid, but a necessary evil if she really wanted to ski.

Her head tilted in interest. "I'll see what Lachlan says. See if we can handle the expense. Or if we can go further into debt with our older sister. She's our not-so-angelic angel investor. But with the amount of sleep Lachlan *isn't* getting these days, I think he'll be happy to throw money at you."

And Asher would be happy to take it.

And to have a reason to see Maggie Reid more often. He might not be in a place to offer more than friendship right now. But she made him smile. And having been in a space where smiles were hard to come by not long ago, he knew better than to squander chances at happiness.

A few hours after the impromptu dog park visit, Maggie let Jackson into her brother's backyard to frolic with Lachlan's dog, and then sneaked in through his front door without knocking.

Well, Lachlan, Marisol and Laura's front door, to be precise. Her brother's summer had been a whirlwind after learning he was going to be a father. He'd fallen in love with Marisol, who'd been in her third trimester of pregnancy. And with Laura's arrival a month ago, he was immersed in the usual infant chaos. No small feat with starting up a new business.

Maggie's chest filled with pride for her little brother. Chronologically little, anyway. As the shrimp in the family, she barely reached Lachlan's armpit. Stella's, too, when their sister wore heels.

She quietly shut the front door and tiptoed up the half flight of stairs to the main floor. Lach had texted to warn her that both Marisol and Laura were napping. She'd have waited until he showed up at work tomorrow to talk to him about hiring Asher, but they were in a hurry.

She hung her purse on the newel post at the top of the stairs. The living room was to her left, anchored by a stone fireplace. Infant paraphernalia decked the warmly decorated space. Her brother lay on his back on the couch with her niece in the crook of his arm. Lachlan was sound asleep. Laura was not. She lay still in her swaddle, her brown eyes wide and blinking.

Maggie went over and stole the baby from her sleeping sibling before going into the adjoining kitchen. "Hello, precious," she cooed, earning Laura's rapt attention.

The baby smacked her lips.

"I can't help you there," she said. "You'll have to talk to your mama about lunch."

She launched into the usual one-sided conversation required of a person holding an infant. Pointing at things in the kitchen and out the back window at the dogs playing on the lawn, singing a little nursery rhyme. Laura was the first infant Maggie had felt any sense of attachment to. She just didn't have the craving to procreate like so many of her friends did. Not that she didn't like kids. Heck, look at Ruth

Matsuda—she was interesting and funny, a genuine delight. But Maggie spent her days trying to solve problems for creatures who couldn't use words. She needed a break from that when she got home.

A floorboard creaked behind her and she turned. Her brother leaned against the counter, rubbing his eyes with the heels of his hands. "You stole my napping buddy."

Laura squirmed and Maggie swayed a little to soothe her. "Only one of you was napping. And you get her all the time."

"All the time, indeed." Lachlan braced himself against the counter for a few seconds before fumbling to get a pod into his coffee maker. "Last night it was at midnight, three and five. Mari's ready to fall over."

Exhaustion permeated his words, but the crinkles around his eyes spoke of a contentment Maggie had never seen on her brother's face before Marisol and Laura. He'd always been a nester. He'd just never had a nest before.

Maggie, however—she kept far away from that kind of intimacy. People like Lachlan and Asher, open to love? They were asking to get hurt.

And Asher…*knowing* it hurt and being willing to do it *again* at some point…

Was he out of his mind?

She stared down at Laura's chubby face. "I hope you stay safe, little one."

Lachlan looked up sharply. "Why wouldn't she?"

Because life doesn't work that way.

Just because her brother had seen the reality of their own fractured family and chose to ignore the possibility of it happening to his relationship didn't mean Maggie had to take the same risk.

"I know you and Marisol will do the best you can, Lach, but even if you're great parents, there's still…"

"Pass me the baby." He held out his hands. "This is a cynicism-free zone."

She shot him a dirty look. "I'm not going to taint your kid."

"You might if you keep spouting doubt all over her precious soul." He snatched his coffee cup off the maker and inhaled. "We aren't destined to replicate Mom and Dad's awful example."

"Says the charmed sibling."

"Says the sibling who's open to possibility," he chided.

Yeah, the possibility of being rejected. Of never feeling good enough. Boarding school, summers away, Christmases spent in either passive-aggressive silence or a barrage of criticism—Maggie's parents had shown her early on it was foolish opening up to someone who could, purposefully or inadvertently, reject her like they had. And the one time she'd ignored that lesson, it had blown up in her face. She'd fallen in love with a guy who worked on the mountain. They'd moved in together, got a puppy together… The puppy he'd taken with him when he up and got a job somewhere in Quebec. No forwarding address.

She still bled inside whenever she treated one of Cleo's three siblings still living in town, now all senior Shepherds with gray muzzles and hearts of gold.

"I'm happy focusing on work, thanks." She dropped a kiss on Laura's forehead. "And being an auntie."

Lachlan shook his head, sighing. "Whatever, Mags. So, why did you interrupt my nap?"

"I have a way to get you more naps. I found someone to do the interior of the barn for us."

"Everyone in town is unavailable," he reminded her. "And either way, the cost would kill our budget."

"Stella will open the purse strings more if necessary." Their older sister raked in money working as a hedge fund manager in New York, and had loaned Lachlan a chunk of cash, despite hating the connection to Sutter Creek. A couple of months back, Lachlan had made the egregious mistake of borrowing money from their dad to make up for an unexpected shortfall right before he'd been scheduled to break ground. Stella had come through instead. Apparently sinking some of her hard-earned savings into Lachlan and Maggie's business was preferable to knowing that her younger siblings owed their emotionally manipulative parents.

"We could call her now," Maggie suggested.

Her brother grimaced. "You don't think she's saved our bacon enough?"

"This is necessary," she said. "Neither of us have time, not if you want it done for your soft open next month."

"Doesn't solve every contractor being booked solid until next year."

She held up a hand. "We don't need a contractor. I found out today that the new librarian has a side hustle."

"Caleb's brother?"

"No, the other new librarian. Of course, Caleb's brother." Caleb Matsuda had only been in Sutter Creek for about a year, but the doctor seemed right at home now, engaged to Maggie's friend Garnet, a lifetime local.

"I guess the guy looks like a construction worker."

That he did. Those biceps…

Side benefit of hiring Asher: she'd get to see him hauling lumber. Over one shoulder.

Just like he could with a lover.

Her belly tingled, a slow burn of possibility…

Would he wear his sexy glasses while hammering, or did he have contacts?

Oh, man. Maybe hiring him was a terrible idea.

Jackson whined at the door to the back porch, a reminder of her priorities. Getting the dog trained and dealing with the dark circles under Lachlan's eyes mattered more than testing her self-control. She could avoid thinking about panty-melting eyewear and straining biceps.

Probably.

"Hey." Her brother snapped his fingers in front of her face. "Space out any harder and you're going to drop my kid." He gently scooped Laura out of Maggie's embrace and tucked the little bundle into the crook of his neck.

"Sorry," she said. "Didn't mean to daydream. Anyway, Asher seemed eager for the work."

"And I like the idea of getting something off my plate."

"Will you call the bank of sister, or shall I?" she said.

"My name's on the loan. I'll do it."

A few minutes later, Stella had confirmed she'd chip in for the extra cost, and they were both breathing easier.

"I'll give Asher a ring." They'd exchanged numbers before leaving the dog park. She couldn't stop her mouth from quirking as the image of his cute, half smile surfaced.

Lachlan raised a brow and jiggled the baby. "Maggie."

He cheeks heated. "What?"

"You're blushing."

"Your sleep deprivation is worse than I thought."

"No, you need to work on your poker face."

She stifled a laugh, then cringed. Damn it, she was grinning like a fool.

Lachlan cupped Laura's swaddled bottom with one hand and pointed a finger at Maggie with the other. "You tittered."

"I did not," she insisted.

"You did. And you're smiling."

"I'm not allowed to smile?"

"Oh, you're allowed. Hell, I'm glad to see you thinking about someone—"

"Shh!"

"Laura's a little young to worry about earmuffs. Besides, Marisol and I want to raise her to know it's good for women to take pleasure—"

"*Lachlan.* For crying out loud, enough!"

Laura squawked.

He pasted on an innocent look before bending his head to his baby's ear and murmuring something in a soothing voice.

"He's telling you lies, Laura," Maggie grumbled.

"Auntie Maggie's just being touchy because she's finally interested in someone, and that scares the snot out of her," her brother said.

"I'm not—*argh*." She stomped into the living room and pulled her phone out of her purse. Swiping in her security pattern, she flopped on the couch, which was still warm from her brother's nap. She dialed Asher's number.

"Maggie Reid," he answered, a smile evident in the greeting. "What can I do you for?"

Oh, you can do me for at least a week.

She cringed. "Crumbs."

"Uh, what?"

Double crumbs. "Oh gosh. I didn't mean... I'm at my brother's, and he was giving me a hard time." Not totally a lie.

"Say no more. I specialize in brotherly angst."

"Giving and receiving, no doubt."

"Oh, no doubt whatsoever. I'm sure if you bought Caleb a drink at the next search and rescue gathering, he'd tell you all sorts of horror stories about the ass pain that is having younger twin brothers."

She laughed.

Lachlan padded into the room and whispered, "Tittering."

She whipped a hand in the air in her brother's direction. "Quiet," she mouthed.

"Quiet?" Asher asked, sounding confused.

Groaning, she dropped her head back on the couch. "I'm so sorry. That was meant to be silent, and for Lachlan."

"Sounds like he's doing a solid pester job. Impressive."

"Sure." She sighed. "Good grief, you're going to think we're nuts. And here I was calling to offer you the job."

"You decided not to because your brother's a pest?" he asked, chuckling a little.

"No. I'm worried you're going to want to steer clear of our family dysfunction."

"Actual dysfunction, or the kind where you blame your siblings for all life's evils but would lay down in the road for them?" he asked, tone thoughtful.

"The latter."

"Then sign me up."

"To...be harassed by my brother?"

He chuckled. "No, to build you some cabinets."

"Right. Cabinets." *Agh*, way to sound intelligent.

"Whatever you need, really."

What she needed was her sense back. "Oh?"

"Flooring, moldings, baseboards—I can do those, too, so long as you have the measurements."

Not quite the need that first came to mind. "Quite a skill range."

"You bet."

Was that suggestion in his voice? What had she been thinking? She'd so teed him up. But he hadn't had to take the shot... Maybe he hadn't. Maybe she was hearing things.

Either way, her chest was getting warm, and that was not okay.

"Uh, Maggie?" Whatever she'd detected in his tone was long gone, replaced by wariness.

"Yes! Right here. Sorry. I—I'm not myself today for some reason." Lachlan snorted, and she glared at him. "We have most of the materials purchased, and the tools, too. What's your hourly rate? "

He named a price that sounded fair to her, then said, "I have some of my own tools. Brought them with me when I moved, figuring I'd need to do home repairs now and again. When do you need the work completed?"

"Lachlan's going to start working classes out of there next month."

Asher whistled. "Doable, I'm sure, but depending on how much needs to be done, and given I'm working with limited hours, I'll want to get to it right away. You're going to be okay with me having to work in spurts?"

"If it means I get Jackson trained up and Lachlan gets more time with his family, you can work at three in the morning for all I care."

He chuckled. "When's your first appointment tomorrow morning?"

"I start at nine on Mondays. And Lach will want to be there, too, of course."

"Naturally. How about I rip by after I drop Ruth at school?" he suggested. "That'll give us twenty minutes, enough time for me to get an idea of what needs doing. And then if I need to pick anything up at the building supply store, I can do it in Bozeman on Tuesday while Ruth's at Hebrew school."

Asher Matsuda, bright and early on a Monday morning? Something fluttered in her stomach. Not butterflies—talk about ridiculous. A crane fly, maybe? Ew. Crane flies were gross. Okay, fine. It was a butterfly. One *solitary* butterfly. "Tomorrow. Sure. See you then."

"Absolutely. I'm looking forward to it, Maggie."

The connection cut, and she stared at her phone. *Gah*. He'd used that tone again. The one that promised he could do more than shelve library books and build cabinets with those big hands of his. She'd noticed his hands this afternoon. His rings had caught her eye. Silver bands around his left middle finger and right ring finger, and a gold one around his right thumb... So freaking attractive...

Aaaaaand the warmth in her chest was back.

Fan-*tastic*.

Lachlan sat down next to her, still cradling the baby to his front. He smirked. "I know that face, Mags. I wore that face all summer."

"You *still* wear a face. But given I'm not interested in seeing anyone, it's not one you'll find on me."

"Not wanting to date and wanting to mess around can coexist."

The skin of her arms prickled at the truth of that, and she scratched both at the same time. "Then all you wanted to do with Marisol was mess around?"

"No, but—"

"So how can it be the same face, then?"

Lachlan grinned. "I know you're trying to reason your way out of a corner here, but all you did was pen yourself into agreeing that you want to get busy with Asher Matsuda."

"I—"

"Ding, ding, ding, the round goes to me." He

stood and headed for the hallway. "It happens so rarely, Maggie. Let me have this one."

The prickles spread across her chest. "But I—"

"I'm going to go savor my sweet victory by napping with my fiancée. Lock the door when you leave."

"Lachlan, you—you—you're the worst!"

His laugh faded with the click of his bedroom door.

Picking up a throw pillow, she pressed it to her face and yelled incoherently into the thick cotton. Whether or not she wanted to get busy with Asher was moot.

He wasn't just passing through town, looking for a short fling like the men she usually dated. He was looking to establish roots—he was a father, for heaven's sake. And he believed he'd find someone to be happy with again.

For his sake, she hoped he did.

But goodness knew, she never had. And never would.

Chapter Three

A fresh twinge of disappointment flickered in Asher's chest as he sat behind the circulation desk of the currently empty library, rereading the text Maggie had sent him before he'd even managed to put on pants this morning.

Maggie: I'm so sorry I can't make it. Assisting with a sticky foal delivery. Up all night. Lach will be there.

He'd met Lachlan alone, and had to admit he'd been sulking for the first couple hours of his Monday shift. Not even working on children's programming helped brighten his mood. He'd figured he could help bridge his way into the community with a few cultural days personal to him. He'd been planning a Tsukimi grass craft that Ruth loved making with his dad for October's full moon, and a day featuring different religious food practices. But this morning, he kept getting distracted. His no worries reply to Maggie had only garnered a Thx in response, and he hadn't heard from her since. She'd be working, so it wasn't like she would have time, but he still wished for more.

Wishes I shouldn't be having anyway. How could he possibly be interested in someone less than two years after losing Alex? Not to mention the look Ruth had given him when she'd accused him of staring at Maggie. His daughter's suspicion was still fresh in his mind. Even if he was starting to feel ready to reenter the dating world, it didn't seem like she approved.

And yet… He'd sure as hell enjoyed springing out of bed before his alarm went off, before he'd found out Maggie wouldn't be able to meet him. Someone had related mourning to the seasons, to a long winter followed by spring. It had seemed an overly trite simile to him at the time, but he could appreciate it a little more now. Coming alive again, regrowth— it rang true. It was refreshing not to have what he'd lost on his mind every moment of the day.

Guilt struck him, and he took a breath. *It's okay to move forward. Necessary, in fact.* Alex had insisted on it. Stage-four lymphoma had been the literal worst in a myriad of ways, but he was grateful as anything for having time with his husband to discuss the future. Alex had hated the idea of Asher being alone, and had insisted that Asher fall in love again when the time was right.

Something to worry about for another day. Right now, he had a daughter to raise and a library to run and a whackload of indoor construction to complete. His meeting with Lachlan, an easygoing guy who shared Maggie's passion for dog training, had gone well. Asher had confirmed he'd have time to build cabinets in Lachlan's office and the classroom, as well as install laminate flooring everywhere except the indoor, cement training ring.

Lachlan had apologized for his sister's absence, too, explaining that living in a rural area, a veterinarian's life wasn't always predictable. Asher had seen that with his twin, though David's urban clinic didn't involve large animals. Maggie's didn't, either, according to her brother, but the horse owner in question was a friend of Maggie's, so she'd gone for moral support and to pitch in if the equine vet needed help.

The clock on Asher's records computer read 11:46 a.m. Surely she'd be done by now. She'd probably be bagged.

Hmm. The library closed for an hour for his lunch on Mondays and Tuesdays; he was the only librarian on staff those days. He could go grab a coffee for Maggie, take it to her at her clinic. Would that be too forward? He didn't want to give her the impression he was looking for anything beyond friendship. But he also really liked her company, and the letdown of not getting to see her this morning...

Given there weren't any patrons at the moment, he pulled up his future sister-in-law's text window on his cell. Garnet was honest to a fault. She also seemed to know Maggie well, so would tell him if this was a terrible idea.

On the scale of "totally platonic" to "I want you to have my babies," where does taking a woman an unsolicited coffee fall?

He sent the message before he lost his nerve.

Three dots floated on the screen for a few seconds before her reply appeared.

Left field, much?

Fair point, he typed before adding, but it doesn't answer my question.

An alert window popped up over his thread with Garnet.

Caleb: You're taking a woman a coffee? Who?

He groaned. He'd assumed his brother would be at work. He tapped Caleb's text and replied:

Piss off, I'm talking to your better half.

By the time he was done sending that, a new message was waiting for him.

Garnet: Depends on the where and why, I guess, but I don't think a coffee is the same as a wedding ring. You're probably safe.

Asher: I'll take probably as definitely. Thanks. And tell C to stop being nosy. He'll know what's going on in my life when there's something that needs knowing.

Slipping his phone into his jeans pocket—the dress code at the branch was pretty casual and let him get away with nice denim—he worked another ten minutes, then locked up and hoofed it the couple of blocks to Peak Beans, one of the shops overlooking the grassy town square.

Sutter Creek's architecture and landscaping couldn't be more different than the brownstones and street-level shops he'd grown up with in Brooklyn. The streets around the square were pedestrian-only. With the summer tourist season over, the raised, wood-planked sidewalks were only scattered with a few people. The buildings were mainly wood faced, too, other than the brick-fronted bank. And the mash-up of old-school-Western and European-ski-town aesthetics was like a Pinterest board that couldn't make up its mind. It was charming, though. And in time, spending a Sunday taking Ruth to the Australian pie place and walking along the creek would feel just as much like home as sharing a mushroom pizza before biking through Prospect Park.

He took his place in line and checked his phone again.

Caleb: Seriously, is there something that needs knowing?

He replied with a no, then sent Garnet another text.

You used to work at the coffee shop in the square, right? Happen to remember what Maggie drinks?

Garnet's and Caleb's identical texts arrived on top of each other. Maggie Reid?

Oh, crap. He'd never hear the end of this. He only acknowledged Garnet's.

She seems like a tea kind of woman, but I'm not sure.

Garnet: Maggie drinks double-shot skim lattes. And doesn't do relationships. So I really hope you're operating on the platonic end of that scale you mentioned.

He exhaled, a wave of something way too close to frustration washing over him. He should have been happy to get that news. All he could have with

Maggie was friendship for the near future, so there was no point in considering something more.

He typed a quick reply to Garnet.

100% friends-only.

And only a small part of him felt like he was lying.

Thank goodness for the love seat tucked into the corner of the staff room, because sitting in an actual chair seemed like an impossible feat at the moment. Maggie let her eyes fall shut, cursing the mere two hours of sleep she'd managed last night before getting called out to her best friend Emma's family ranch to help out with an insanely difficult birth of a foal. *Not birth. Death.* Her eyes stung, hot and sharp. She pressed the heels of her hands against her lids. She'd mainly gone for Emma's sake, though once things got hairy the equine vet had appreciated the second set of hands.

Maggie didn't usually get upset to the point of tears over a lost animal, but Emma and her mom had both fallen apart, and in her exhaustion, Maggie had, too. And for whatever reason, was having trouble putting herself back together.

Having a dog-sitting foal was super rare, enough that Maggie had only read about it in journal articles. The other vet had been compassionate but

pragmatic—there wasn't anything that could have prevented it from happening, nor allowed for a live birth.

We saved the mare. At least we managed that.
But it didn't seem like enough, not for Emma and
her mom, who loved their animals like family. Maggie would have done anything to be able to help deliver a live foal.

"Frick, why?" she complained to the empty room.

"Good question."

The male voice, not her brother's or her receptionist's, made her jump enough that her butt left the
couch for a second. She dropped her hands from her
eyes and turned to the intruder.

Asher Matsuda's big frame filled the doorway.
He had on jeans and yet another pair of super sexy
boots. He'd pushed up the sleeves of his thin, striped
sweater, revealing his strong forearms. He held a
to-go coffee cup in each hand. His apologetic smile
eased the warning bells clanging in her chest. "I'm
sorry. I should have been louder, avoided startling
you. Your receptionist directed me back here. Well,
first he invited me to join the local LGBTQ+ rock
climbing club—he and his boyfriend apparently run
it? Might take him up on that after I finish this job
for you and your brother. Ruth isn't the only one
who needs to get out of the house… Anyway, my
agreement seemed to be the magic ticket, because
he waved me in your direction. And now I've totally talked your ear off. Just what you needed."

He walked into the room, gaze darting between the empty seat beside her and the kitchen table and chairs centering the space. "Can I sit?"

"Sure," she said. Not like he was going to plunk down next to her when there were six perfectly good chairs—

He strode the last few steps and settled onto the empty love seat cushion. Her own cushion tilted from the shift in weight. She had to right herself to avoid touching shoulders with him.

But she wasn't going to be rude and ask him to move, not when he was so kindly holding out one of the disposable cups to her.

"I checked with Garnet to see what you drank," he said.

"You did?" Crumbs, that was going to require some explanation. She took the beverage and held it with both hands. The warmth cut through the chill of her skin. She shivered. Adrenaline letdown always dragged on longer for her than it did most people. Happened with work emergencies and her search and rescue volunteering.

"Figured you needed some caffeine, and I didn't want to get you the wrong thing," he explained.

"That was nice of you," she said lamely.

He lifted a shoulder. "Your brother mentioned you had a rough night. Night *and* morning."

A lump formed in her throat. "How did the walk-through go?"

"Fine." Worry marked his dark brown eyes. "*You* don't look fine, though."

She bit her lip. "Sorry. I don't usually get this upset about work. But with the horse being my best friend's... Hard not to feel that I failed her. Silly, really—I'm not even an equine vet, nor was I in charge."

"Lachlan mentioned this particular scenario involved a whole lot of unpleasantness."

"I—yeah. Not exactly fun. Way too many saws involved to inflict the grim details on laypeople."

He switched his drink from his right to his left hand and reached for her leg, but pulled back at the last second and settled his big palm on his own knee. "Between my parents and Caleb being doctors and Dave's veterinary practice, it's a rare family dinner that doesn't involve some crazy medical case. Not much fazes me, Maggie."

Bemusement tugged the corners of his mouth up.

Oh, sweet baby jellybeans. That smile could melt a glacier, let alone an under-slept woman with way too much of a soft spot for thick-rimmed glasses and running her fingers through beards...

"My parents have always given Lachlan a hard time for not accumulating as many degrees as Stella and me," she explained. "Were your parents the same?"

"Not at all," he said. "They cheered just as loudly from the front row when my band played as they did at Caleb's and Dave's convocations. Sure, my mom's a big fan of me being a librarian now, but that's mainly because she loves books. And after Alex's first bout with cancer, she wanted me to have a more reliable paycheck."

"Was Alex—" She coughed, trying to remove the lump that had been half clogging her throat since she left RG Ranch. None of the questions that came to mind were any of her business. "Never mind."

"It's okay." His voice cracked a little. "The more people who know who Alex was, the more there is of him still in the world."

"Asher…"

"What am I saying, though? You've dealt with death enough today."

Her nose stung. Yeah, the morning had left bruises on her soul, but Asher's were infinitely worse. "I'm happy to listen. Well, not happy. Because it's obviously the most tragic thing you could go through, and—oh, for crying out loud." Her cheeks heated. "You should be the one talking, not me."

Talking? Try babbling. Good work, Maggie.

His bemused smile eased a little of her embarrassment. "He had cancer twice as an adult."

"Oh…"

Bracing his fingers on his coffee cup, he stared at the black plastic lid. "He was a decade older than me." The corner of his lips twitched. "I was so infatuated by the idea of an older partner. Anyway, we'd been dating for about three years—I was twenty-two. He was pretty on top of his health. Caught his thyroid cancer early. We went on with our lives."

She did a bit of mental math based on knowing Caleb was almost forty and Asher was a few years younger. "You must have had Ruth not long after."

He nodded. "Alex didn't want to risk biological fatherhood because of his rounds of radiation and chemo, but his cousin in Connecticut was willing to be our surrogate with me as donor. All very clinical, that part. But we ended up with Ruth. Which… science is the best. She's been nothing less than amazing since the day she was born. Parenting and marriage were a little out of order and complicated by a hell of a lot of paperwork and red-tape—and, let's be honest, bigotry at times—but it was worth it."

"Quite the journey."

"Mmm-hmm. We weren't expecting the lymphoma, though. We knew he faced a higher risk, but once he reached five years cancer-free, we really thought it wasn't coming back."

Tears stung her eyes again. Now it was her turn to want to reach for him, to lay a hand on his leg or arm so he knew she was hearing his pain. Her brain clamored to hold back, but she ignored the warning. She squeezed his bare forearm. His skin was warm against her fingers.

Surprise lit his eyes. He settled his palm over the back of her hand. "You, uh… Your hand is cold."

"Takes me forever to shed my adrenaline response," she said. "Plus being tired."

He studied her face, his expression serious. "You don't cancel your appointments when you've been up all night?"

"Not always. I wouldn't be able to sleep, anyway." Despite her exhaustion, she might need to rely on some melatonin tonight to keep away the visions of the grim surgery she'd witnessed.

"Well, drive safe when you're on your way home."

Her fingers were finally warm, sandwiched between his arm and palm. Did he realize he was essentially holding her hand?

Not that she cared either way. So long as he didn't let go...

No, Maggie, you need to let go. *Before he figures out you don't really want to.*

She slid her fingers out from his and forced a smile. Standing, she straightened her scrubs and took another drink of coffee. "I live literally across the street, so as long as I look both ways and don't fall asleep on the yellow line, I'll be okay." She lifted the beverage. "And this'll go far. Thank you so much."

He smiled back and rose to his feet. Oh my, he was tall. And broad.

And everything else you can't afford to notice.

She'd tried not to be cynical once. Told herself relationships could work, that they weren't all cheating and lies like her parents' marriage. She'd forced herself to be vulnerable, found a man who shared her hobbies and loved animals… Hadn't loved her, though. She'd gotten home from work the day to find he'd abruptly left. Losing him had broken her heart. Losing Cleo had been like losing part of her soul. And she'd learned never to ignore her instincts again.

Instincts that never stopped shouting for her to keep her distance from love.

"When will you be starting the work?" she croaked.

"Wednesday evening. See you then?" He backed away a few steps.

"Oh, likely," she said, waving as he smiled, saluted casually and headed for the hallway.

She couldn't exactly avoid her workplace. But unless she was able to shed the desire to wrap her arms around his wide shoulders and cling to him until the emotional remnants of her long night faded, she'd best find somewhere else to be when he came back, hammer in hand.

Chapter Four

Maggie lit out of work as if she had a rampaging grizzly on her tail after her shifts on both Wednesday and Thursday, successfully managing to avoid Asher when he came in to work on the barn. And Friday night and Saturday weren't an issue since he took that time off.

By Sunday, she was about to declare a ghosting victory for the week, when a client called her cell, interrupting her post-lunch attempts to train Jackson in her backyard.

"Maggie! Thank you for picking up, dear. I just— I'm in a pickle, and I need your help."

Gertie Rafferty was a longtime Sutter Creek

local and one of the more community-minded seniors in town. She was also Lachlan's landlord, and the grandmother of Stella's jerk of an ex-boyfriend. Maggie chose to ignore that particular connection just now.

"I'm just training Jackson, Mrs. Rafferty. What can I do for you?"

Gertie cleared her throat. "I was training Kittay to use the toilet, you see…"

"Uh, the litter box?"

"No, the toilet. I saw it on the internet, and it looked like an excellent idea. Now that we're in the senior's living community, I figured it better to have one less thing to clean up."

"I'm afraid I've never trained a cat to use a toilet, Mrs. Rafferty. And it goes against feline instinct, so it's not—"

"That's not the problem, dear. Kittay got stuck in the toilet."

Maggie stopped dead. "Say what?"

"She caught on quick like a bunny. Was on a streak of using it for a week straight. But then… She fell in. And it must have sent the water level high enough to trigger the auto flush, because I heard this awful yowling, and when I went into the bathroom, Kittay's hind leg was down the crapper."

"I—" Maggie cleared her throat. This was certainly a first. "Were you able to get her out? Does she need care?"

"Well, I called my grandson."

Maggie held in a growl at the mention of the Sutter Creek sheriff. He'd get some ribbing about this one at the station. Good. His long-ago actions meant Maggie and Lachlan had been limited to a long-distance relationship with their older half-sister since high school. Ryan Rafferty deserved every bit of grief thrown his way. "Did the sheriff have any success?"

"Kittay was too wound up to let him get near. Scratching his arms into ribbons. We called in the fire department."

And no doubt guaranteed themselves a spot on the front page of the *Sutter Creek Sentinel*.

"Mrs. Rafferty—" as much as this story was bound to be recited in the streets and pews for the next weeks, and Maggie had first access to it, she really needed to prioritize the health of her patient "—did the fire department get the cat out? Does Kittay need veterinary care?"

"Well, it took some time, but they did manage to free her. And I know we're supposed to go to the emergency clinic in Bozeman on your days off, but I'm afraid putting Kittay in a carrier for the car ride would right do her in. Could I impose—"

"Of course. I'll meet you at the clinic in ten minutes." So much for having all of Sunday off. And so much for keeping her distance from the hot librarian who kept popping into her thoughts at the most inconvenient times. After hanging up, she stashed away the noisemakers she'd been using to try to condition Jackson and put a hand between his shoulder blades. "Come on, buddy, time to go to work."

He stood at attention.

She shook her head. He was so darn good at this part of being a service animal. But her attempts to work with him on his fear of noise were not going as well. She'd planned to spend her day working up to his desensitization training. With any luck, whatever attention Kittay needed wouldn't steal too much time away from their schedule. She clipped Jackson's short leash on his collar and they trudged across the road. "Maybe if we go through the front, Asher won't notice we're here. We can get in and out quick."

The dog cocked his blocky head.

"Oh, you don't think we can be stealthy? I know I can," she said to him, letting herself in the front door. Asher was up to his ears in laminate, according to Lachlan's reports. Hopefully he'd keep to the back building.

After a thorough examination, she determined Kittay was freaked right out, but hadn't suffered any injuries. She escorted Mrs. Rafferty and the unhappy, carrier-bound cat back to the front reception area.

The bell dinged, and thudding footsteps entered the room. Crud, Asher had—

She glanced up and her heart sank. Not Asher. Ryan Rafferty. She couldn't decide what was worse.

Asher challenged her willpower, but Ryan brought back echoes of her sister's tears. Especially when he was dressed in cowboy getup, as opposed to his sheriff's uniform. *Gah.* How many times had she seen her sister jump in Ryan's truck and melt all over his bad-boy-on-the-range self? Only to have Ryan toss Stella's heart out the window when he got in that truck and took off for the other side of the state after a teenage run-in with the law. He'd never responded when Stella tried to contact him to tell him she was pregnant. Or that she'd miscarried.

Yet another reason why Maggie had been reluctant to get into a relationship, and why getting walked out on herself had been extra painful—she should have known better. A short, sex-only fling was okay now and again, but dating someone just wasn't worth the risk. Not even a seemingly nice guy like Asher. If she let herself dip her toes into the pool of temptation, she'd end up drowning again.

She fixed a neutral, professional expression on her face and nodded at the sheriff. "Good afternoon."

"Hey, Maggie." His smile faded. He took the cat carrier from Mrs. Rafferty and gave the older woman a quick hug. "The truck's open, Gran."

Mrs. Rafferty thanked Maggie again and left out the front door.

Ryan, for whatever reason, stayed behind.

Maggie stood behind the desk and crossed her arms. It was always a fine balance with the sheriff. She couldn't forget his past with Stella, no matter how long ago it had happened. Her loyalty lay with her sister. But Sutter Creek was a small town, and both Maggie and Lachlan worked with Ryan on search and rescue operations. The sheriff was the technical head of SAR operations in the county, so as much as she wanted to snub the man, she couldn't compromise their professional connection. "What can I do for you?"

"Thanks for humoring my grandmother," he said, tone as tentative as an arrogant, self-involved law enforcement officer's could be.

"I wasn't humoring her. Kittay could have had significant joint damage."

He rubbed the back of his neck. "I guess. I appreciate you coming in on the weekend either way."

She stared at him. Why wasn't he getting the memo that he wasn't welcome here? Did he forget what he'd done, stealing a key part of her family? With their parents never providing a warm and loving home in Chicago, Maggie and Lachlan had depended on their summers in Sutter Creek to be their foundation, their chance at normalcy with their grandparents and older half-sister. But when a heartbroken Stella had vowed never to return and took off for the East Coast, Maggie and Lachlan lost their close relationship with her. Stella hadn't only cut Ryan out of her life, she'd thrown up walls with her siblings, too.

The silence must have grown uncomfortable enough for Ryan to have to break it, because he said, "I—uh—I heard Stella's investing in the expansion."

"News travels," she said, teeth gritted.

"Do you think she'll be coming for a visit, then?" Faint hope lit his eyes.

Well, it was her job to crush that hope to dust. "You don't get to ask about her, Sheriff."

"I know, but, Maggie—"

"But nothing. You're good at your job, and I respect that. And I'll take orders from you during any SAR incident when we're both on scene. But I'm not discussing Stella. And we're not going to be friends."

He exhaled, a frustrated noise that filled the otherwise empty waiting room. "Let me know if we can change that at some point."

Turning on a heel, he trudged out.

She was about to lock up when a throat cleared behind her. She jumped and let out a truly pathetic shriek. Spinning, she took in the burly frame of the man standing in the hall that ran perpendicular to the front desk. His hands were jammed into his worn jeans.

Putting a hand over her thrumming heart, she took a breath and squeaked out, "Asher!"

He sent her an apologetic smile. "Thought you heard me come in."

"Clearly not." Oh man. Cotton T-shirts everywhere were probably begging for the opportunity to grace this man's shoulders. He'd trimmed his beard, and the hitch at the corner of his mouth… A little knowing, a little nervous, a whole lot sexy.

Gah. Those shoulders, that mouth—they were not for her enjoyment. She really needed to keep it friendly.

But the flutter in her belly was not getting the memo. She steeled herself, fighting the silly, instinctive smile that wanted free.

"Third time's a charm," he said.

She lifted a brow in question. "What do you mean?"

He took his hands out of his pockets and crossed his arms, and good gracious, that made the ropes of muscle in his forearms bulge in spectacular ways. "You weren't here either Wednesday or Thursday."

"I wasn't. I was, uh, out training Jackson." That was truthful enough. She didn't need to explain that the reason she'd taken the dog elsewhere was to avoid having to look into Asher's dark brown eyes and feel things she shouldn't be feeling. "Good thing Jackson's napping in the back room. You would have scared the daylights out of him."

"Instead, I scared you," he said.

Heat spilled into her cheeks. "Startled. A little."

His lips twitched. "If that's what we're calling it these days."

She lifted her chin. "We are."

"So, uh, who was the guy? An ex?"

"I don't date," she snapped.

One of his dark brows raised in a wary arc. "Apologies for hitting a button. I just wanted to make sure you're safe."

She inhaled through her nose. "Sorry. Forgot that you're not a local. You wouldn't be privy to my life history. That was the sheriff. My *sister's* ex."

"Being in law enforcement doesn't necessarily mean he's safe." Asher's serious tone was so darn soothing. As was his caution. Her pulse slowed from her earlier anger at Ryan and being startled by Asher.

"He's not a physical danger," she said.

"Which isn't the only kind of safety that matters."

And by saying and knowing that, Asher was all the more fascinating to Maggie, pushing her that much further into the danger zone.

She backed up a few steps until her rear hit the desk. She glanced pointedly at the clock on the wall. "It's my day off. I should really get out of here." If she left now, she could put in three hours of training and playtime before dinner.

His face fell. "Oh. I was going to ask you for a favor. But if you have to go, don't worry about it."

Curiosity piqued, she sighed. "What do you need? Someone to hold the tape measure?"

He smiled sheepishly. "No, I've conscripted Ruth for that. But she's been really patient today, and I want to get another hour of work done. I was wondering if she could hang out with your dog."

"Well, I—"

"Sorry, you probably have plans. You weren't even supposed to be in today, were you?"

"It's always something. Today happened to be a cat flushing itself down a toilet." She smiled, just a small one. If she gave him more than that, she might be tempted to give him even more still.

The corner of his mouth twitched. "With intent?"

"There were no witnesses."

He chuckled. "Is that why the law showed up? Taking the cat into custody for self-harm?"

Had the law enforcement officer in question not shattered her sister's heart, she would have laughed, too.

"Nah. But the fire department got called."

"Oh man. A story destined to make the rounds," he said. "By the time I open the branch tomorrow, I'll have three people telling me they heard the fire-fighters had to give the cat CPR, and extracted the entire toilet from the house, and it took the Jaws of Life to finally rescue the poor feline."

She smiled fully. With teeth, almost. Shoot. But she couldn't help it. She could see him standing be-hind the circulation desk in a dress shirt and jeans, looking sexier than any person deserved to look, humoring a stream of patrons as they spread exag-gerated tales of Kittay's trauma. "You've got Sutter Creek figured out."

"I hope so."

His eagerness hit her right in the chest. It was

impossible to miss how he liked the quirkiness that made the small town home. Given she wasn't ever going to make a family with a partner, being a part of the community, no matter its overbearing moments, gave her a place. And Asher seemed to want that, too, for him and Ruth.

And I could help with that. With friendship, that is.

"I have to put in a few hours with the dog this afternoon to make up for losing time here," she said. "But maybe Ruth can give me a hand with desensitization training. She can make noises for me." The invitation spilled out, unwanted but impossible to take back. No matter. She could figure out a way to ignore the curling heat in her belly for the sake of helping this man and his daughter feel like they were a part of the town. "And I was planning to take him for a walk down Main Street later, if you want to come with."

He grinned. "I think we can make that work."

A couple of hours later, Asher wiped the sweat and sawdust off his face and forearms with a rag he'd tucked in the back pocket of his jeans. He was using the main space of the barn as his work area, what Lachlan had explained would be the indoor training and multipurpose area. But for now, it was a cement-floored, empty-walled, square room, about half the size of a small tennis court. A safe enough space for Ruth, as all the major construction work was done and she knew the rules about being safe around power tools and stacks of supplies. Boring for her, though. Asher was halfway through installing the flooring in the office spaces and classroom. The cabinet work would take longer, so he had weeks left of Ruth's long sighs. He'd emphasized how this would mean skiing soon, and she was on board, but hanging around watching her dad do construction work wasn't exactly riveting.

Hopefully Maggie didn't mind having Ruth pitch in with the dog. They'd vacated for the yard once he turned on the circular saw. The dog had nearly hit the ceiling at that noise.

After cleaning up his work site, he headed outside to find his daughter. He was sorely tempted by Maggie's invitation for a walk, but would he be outstaying his welcome?

At least he knew she wasn't looking for a deep connection of any kind. Her "I don't date" had been pretty damn clear. Which lined up nicely with his commitment to keeping Ruth's and his life simple.

The part of him that wanted to stare at Maggie's dancing smile and lithe form all damn day would just have to piss off.

He stepped onto the grass, and a hundred-and-fifty-plus pounds of Great Dane galloped toward him like the world's most ungainly white-tailed deer. Jackson wasn't wearing his vest, and a chew rope dangled from one side of his mouth.

"Hey, buddy." He scratched the dog's ears and got a full-body lean in return that rocked him back on his heels. Catching his balance, he grinned at Ruth, who stood across the lawn with Maggie.

Maggie smacked her hands against her jeans-covered thighs to call the dog back. "Jackson, come."

A brilliant smile split his daughter's lips as she motioned for the dog to drop the rope and then tossed it, sending the beast gamboling across the lawn again.

His heart squeezed at the joy on Ruth's face, and he strolled over.

"Liking that smile, peanut." He took in Maggie, her blond curls bouncing around her face. "Thanks so much for including Ruth."

"She was a big help," Maggie said. "Did you decide on the walk?"

He hadn't needed to decide—his daughter's happiness did it for him. Even if it meant hiding how, in an ideal world, he'd be more interested in an adults-only date. "Yeah, we're up for that. As long as we find some ice cream on the way."

A half hour later, Asher handed Maggie her raspberry cheesecake swirl cone. Her appreciative smile hit him square in the chest, and he almost stumbled back against the waist-high counter from the impact. Man, this woman's smile could shake the earth.

And all his good intentions.

He mentally steeled himself and smiled back.

"Thank you," she said, Jackson in his vest at her side as she waded through the Sunday afternoon crowd in the ice-cream shop, Gallatin Gelato. "You have good taste in flavors."

He raised his own double scoop—the same flavor as hers—and held the door open for her. No reason to read anything into coincidentally ordering identical treats—it wasn't that odd a choice. "Too many good options. Ruth and I might have to make a weekend habit of coming here so I can try them all."

He and Ruth followed Maggie as she turned right along the town center's raised sidewalk. Ruth was quiet, busy enjoying her blue bubble gum scoop nestled in a waffle cone.

"I'd say your waistline would complain from repeat visits," Maggie said, "but you don't look like you have to think about that." A second after casually tossing that out, she stumbled on the wood planking. Jackson went on the alert, nudging her ankle and freezing in place.

"You okay?" Asher asked, chest warming a little that she'd admitting to paying attention to his physique.

She reddened, and he got the distinct impression that her stumble hadn't been a training exercise. Had she not meant to give him the compliment, either? It had been fairly offhand. Maybe she hadn't meant it as anything but an observation.

"I'm fine," she said. She praised the dog and

started walking again. They spent a few minutes strolling along the sidewalk with Ruth leading the way. Maggie pointed out some of the stores in the vicinity.

"The town should hire you as a tour guide," he said.

Her cheeks pinked again, matching the swirl of raspberry in her cone. "I used to work for the Chamber of Commerce during the summer. Old habits die hard."

"No, I appreciate it. I mean, Caleb and Garnet have shown me around a few times, but it never hurts to have another perspective. Got any leads on used ski equipment for kids? Garnet's employee discounts don't extend to her fiancé's niece, so she can't help with Ruth's ski costs as much as I'd hoped."

"Yeah, Skis and Spokes runs a consignment program." She waved her free hand at a large storefront anchoring one of the four sides of the town square. The pedestrian-only area, four streets framing a pristine lawn, buzzed with activity, despite it being the early October shoulder season.

"That'd be perfect. What do you say, Ruth— should we check out some skis next Saturday?" Next Shabbat was an off week for their small synagogue in Bozeman. His beliefs didn't run as deeply as his mother's did or Alex's had, but Ruth had really benefited from the community and rituals since Alex's death. Asher made it a priority to attend services whenever possible.

Her face lit up even more than when she'd been playing with Jackson and he'd suggested ice cream. "Seriously, Daddy?"

"Of course. As long as you can keep being patient while I get the finishing work done, we can start looking at getting you up on the hill. We'll have to wait to figure out the ski team, but Garnet's happy to give you lessons once the season starts, regardless."

Ruth frowned. "Oh. Not the team."

"Not yet." His gut pinched. He had no problem saying no to his daughter when it had to do with setting healthy boundaries, but having to deny her a new athletic activity made him question his parenting abilities. "I'll see how much money I manage to save while working on the barn."

"I know, Dad." She trudged ahead, glancing longingly at a high-end sporting goods store window as they passed.

A flash of turquoise, Ruth's favorite color, caught his eye from the window display. The snow jacket looked to be her size. Maybe if it went on sale at some point, he'd see about getting it for her birthday in January. But that was something to deal with later. Right now, he was far more interested in getting closer to the woman walking alongside him. The breeze fluttered around them, sending little whiffs of her scent his way, and damn, she smelled like a dream. "Jackson seems a hundred percent in tune with you."

She blew out a breath. Her knuckles whitened around the dog's short lead. "He's awesome as a support dog. But you saw him today with the noise from the saw. I'm running out of ways to help him over his fear."

He hated the defeat in her tone. "That sucks, Maggie. What's your next step?"

"Sound recording therapy. But I dunno. If he hasn't responded already..." Her lips screwed up tight for a second. "Failing is the worst."

"Grandpa says that if we fall down seven times, stand up eight," Ruth said offhandedly before taking a big lick of her bright blue ice cream cone. "And Papa told me failing's part of learning."

Maggie's mouth twitched from disappointment to amused. "That's solid advice."

"Alex was a teacher," Asher said. "Infinitely more patient and wise than I am."

To the point where, in his lowest moments, his blackest grief, he wondered why in the world it had been Alex to die rather than himself. That Ruth would have been better off... But it didn't do much good dwelling on life's mysteries. He'd just follow Alex's advice and do his best. And learn any time he screwed up.

"Sounds like your Papa was a pretty great guy,"

Maggie said to Ruth. "Which doesn't surprise me, because you're a rather lovely kid."

"Thank you," Ruth said, a hint of "I know" coloring her tone. She'd been praised lavishly since she was a baby, so she accepted it as truth. "Maggie, I was wondering…"

"Dr. Reid," he murmured.

"Maggie said I could use her first name, Dad."

Oh, the beleaguered tone of a preteen. "Excellent. Just checking."

"Anyway," Ruth continued, dark eyes growing serious. "What happens… Well… What happens if Jackson *doesn't* get used to noises?"

Maggie paused as they crossed the street to the green space, clearly weighing her words. "Well, the organization I'm training him for will rehome him."

Ruth stiffened. "You're not going to keep him?"

"He's not mine to keep."

"Well, that's the worst," Ruth announced. "Oh!" She perked up. "There's Harper. Can I go say hi?"

"Of course," he said.

She sprinted across the lawn, skirting the gazebo, a frilly, pastel-painted structure reminiscent of the Cape Cod houses they'd rented as a family on summer vacations. It had been a tradition from his childhood that he and Alex had kept up as parents, up until Alex got too sick to travel.

"She's delightful, Asher," Maggie said, gaze tracking his bounding daughter. Jackson looked longingly in Ruth's direction, but stayed close to Maggie's side.

"I like to think so."

"Says a lot about you."

He shrugged. "It's all guesswork. And following my parents' example."

Her forehead furrowed. "Can't say my parents provided any parenting skills I'd want to mimic."

"Sorry to hear that."

She sighed. "I don't want kids of my own, so it's moot."

Yeah, he doubted that. Deciding not to have kids was fine and good, but growing up with crappy parents sure wasn't. He'd experienced that intimately with Alex's family. And Maggie deciding to open up intrigued him. A change from her guardedness, from how she'd so obviously been avoiding him. How much time would it take to fully break through the wall she had built up? But that wasn't the right way to look at it. He cringed at the thought of breaking something about her, even if it was a metaphor. Talk about exactly what Alex's parents had tried to do to their son. No, any leeway into Maggie Reid's psyche would have to be freely offered up. An autumn project, perhaps. Convince her he was trustworthy.

He'd start with some semi-common ground. "I wasn't sure about parenthood, myself. I could have gone either way. But Alex loved kids—I was happy to follow his lead. And Ruth, well… Can't ask for a better child."

She nodded. "Don't get me wrong, I love kids when they're older, but I'm not maternal around babies."

"No judgment here." He held up his hands. "I had lots of kid-free friends in Brooklyn. And I can't say the infant stage was my favorite part of fatherhood. Ruth keeps getting more fun the older she gets."

"A bonus to living in the city—far more people who aren't hitched and procreating." She motioned toward the groupings of families tossing Frisbees and lounging on the grass. "Even though Sutter Creek has its fair share of seasonal employees, the core is pretty two-parent, three-point-four-kid based. I'm an outlier."

She was? She'd had conversations with about eight different people while they'd been waiting for their ice cream. "You seem pretty tied to the town."

"Oh, I am. Sutter Creek is in my blood. Through my grandparents, that is—I can probably count on one hand the number of times my parents have been here in the past twenty years. They haven't even come to meet Laura yet. Stella hasn't, either. And that's not the kind of person or neighbor I want to be. I just meant that being single and not being a mom doesn't really fit the mold."

"Better to break the mold than force yourself into it," he said. "Trying to live a lie eventually hurts more than it does to live outside everyone's expectations."

She raised a brow and corrected Jackson when he sidestepped too far from her hip. "A personal lesson?"

"Yeah. The assumptions people make about me being bi never fail to amaze." Fortunately, he'd been born to accepting, open parents. His road hadn't been quite as bumpy to travel as some of the journeys of his friends back in New York, but had still had its challenges. He'd started to think about coming out at eighteen, first wondering if he was gay, then being told by a school counsellor that it was likely just a phase because he'd had a girlfriend. For a while he'd believed there was something entirely wrong with him before he finally broke down in front of his mom. She'd talked things out with him, had accepted him, helped him to accept himself. Having a safe retreat had made it easier when people questioned him about when he was going to pick a side or assuming he was attracted to every living, breathing human on the planet.

Maggie blew out a breath. "Learning to be true to yourself isn't exactly painless, though."

"No, not at all," he agreed. "Didn't magically get easier with age, either. Alex and I had to accept that our love meant never having a relationship with his parents. Not the easiest thing to explain to Ruth. But we decided living life—rejecting hate—was the best example to set for her."

"They… But…" Her mouth fell open.

"Don't worry about defining it. There aren't the right words."

"Do people give her a hard time?"

"Sometimes about having two dads, sometimes about her ethnicity. Depends on where we are. She's pretty resilient most of the time. More than I was at her age." He waved at his daughter, who was halfway across the lawn, skipping in his direction.

She came to a halt, cheeks pink and eyes bright. "Harper asked me over for dinner. Can I go?"

"What are they having, love?"

"Cheeseburgers. But I can ask to keep the cheese off," she said hurriedly, smile wobbling.

He nodded at his daughter's attempt to fit their eating habits in with her social life. "Okay. Just do your best. And be honest with whoever is cooking dinner if you need to. If there aren't enough options, you can eat when you get home. We have leftover udon in the fridge." He turned to Maggie. "Be back in a minute."

He walked Ruth back to her friend and confirmed details with Harper's dad, who seemed unfazed by the particularities of Ruth's diet.

Asher left his daughter to make friends. Was that what he was doing with Maggie? Making friends?

He couldn't tell if his jittering nerves were from leaving Ruth with a new family or from the time alone with Maggie.

She was doing a big loop around the grassy square with the dog, practicing training maneuvers and occasionally having to calm him when he got spooked. He made it back to her side just as she was rising from a simulated fall like the one in the library that he'd thought was real.

She brushed off her knees and cocked a blond brow. "I'm ignorant on this one—cheeseburgers aren't kosher?"

"Nope. No milk and meat in the same meal," he answered.

"*Huh.* I feel I should have known that, given I've eaten at your brother's house a few times."

He lifted a shoulder. "Caleb's nonobservant. And I'm not a hundred percent. Other than on holidays, we only keep a kosher-style kitchen. Alex and I decided it was enough to strike a balance."

She nodded. "Well, you're safe at my house. I'm vegetarian—my kitchen's been meat-free since I bought the place from my grandfather a few years back."

That was close to an invitation—

Close, but not exactly. She isn't interested in you coming over.

Nor could he afford to wish she was. Best to keep things in friend mode. "I'll remember that if we're ever at a group function—I'll bring something vegetarian friendly."

"Thank you, I—" She coughed, blushing. "Are you going to finish up more work on the barn? Now that you're free and easy for a few hours?" Her gaze darted to the dog, who stood at her side, intent on his task. Her hand tightened on his lead.

"I will. But I'll probably grab something to eat first." No time like the present to work on trying to get her to relax a little more. Friends could share a meal out, after all. "Feel like joining me?"

"Sorry. I need to keep working with Jackson." She tugged on her lip with her teeth. "You'll be at the barn on Tuesday? With Ruth?"

"By myself," he explained. "She has Hebrew school that afternoon. Caleb's going to take her to Bozeman—he has some errands to run."

"Do you like Thai food?"

"Love it." Loved where this was going, too.

"Tofu pad Thai okay? And veggie green curry?"

Warmth bloomed in his belly and he grinned. "Absolutely."

"I'll grab takeout. See you then." Dropping a quick goodbye, she jogged off, the dog loping at her side.

He barely had time to say goodbye, or to thank her for the tour around the square before she was out of earshot. And her impulsive offer had seemed to surprise her as much as it had him. But something about her determination made him believe that, unlike last week, when she promised she'd see him at work, she'd follow through.

Chapter Five

After seeing her last patient on Tuesday, Maggie ran out to retrieve the takeout she'd promised Asher. Jackson stared at her from his harnessed spot in the crew cab of her truck, his brown eyes communicating some sort of deep sorrow in the reflection of the rearview mirror. That, or he wanted to dig into the pad Thai sitting in a paper bag on the floorboard of the front passenger seat.

"What, buddy?"

"Ah-roo," he warbled.

"Oh, talkative today?"

"Ah-roo-roo."

"Sorry, food's not for you. It's for Asher and me."

She glanced at the mirror again and swore he narrowed his eyes. "What?"

He looked to the side and let out a huff.

"Asher is just a friend. I'm feeding an employee." Though the fact she felt it necessary to explain herself to a four-legged fur giant spoke volumes. And if she was having to explain it to a dog, was the situation unclear enough that Asher might be getting the wrong message?

She really needed to talk to a human being. Garnet wouldn't work—Asher was essentially her brother-in-law. And Lachlan would totally assume the wrong thing, as would her best friend, Emma. She needed someone who was less of a romantic.

Dictating Marisol's number to her in-vehicle call system, she crossed her fingers that her brother's fiancée was awake.

Marisol answered on the second ring with a big yawn. "Please say you're calling to offer babysitting services."

She laughed. "I wasn't, but I'm happy to. How about Friday evening? Jackson has his test that afternoon, but I could watch Laura in the evening. You and Lach could go out for dinner or something."

"A real meal out?" The wonder in Marisol's voice wasn't doing anything to sell parenthood. "Like, with cutlery and not consumed standing over the kitchen counter?"

"Life with an infant is that awesome, is it?"

"Life with an infant is the most incredible thing in the world," Marisol replied. "For us, anyway."

"I'm happy that you and Lach are made to be parents." And for each other. She still couldn't figure out how that had happened, given how danged rare it was for two people to find each other and actually be suited and actually want the same things in life, but her brother had always had that extra magic about him. Even when dealing with all their parents' garbage, he'd kept his optimism. "And having some Auntie-and-kiddo time will be fantastic."

She could either celebrate Jackson's successful desensitization with her niece, or distract herself from his failure.

Her own failure.

The beginnings of a lump teased her throat. Staying upbeat when he still had so far to go was becoming impossible.

"How's Jackson doing?" Marisol asked.

Marisol was a PhD student in canine psychology, so they'd had many a discussion about techniques and strategies. "He's showing some improvement, but not enough. He needs to be a rock, and he just... isn't." She sent him an apologetic look in the rearview mirror. "Sorry, buddy."

"I'd say he'll catch on, but Maggie—it might be too late. Not all dogs are made for life in a service profession."

"No need to tell me that. I know the stats." But

he'd be an F on her perfect record, and that chafed at every cell of her being. Especially since he was such a sweetheart. "So, I have a question for you."

"About the dog?" Marisol said. "I think I shared everything I could think of."

"No, about a guy."

"Gotta say, that's way more interesting. Tell me about things beyond diapers and nap schedules."

Maggie snorted. "Give me a break. My brother was wooing you all summer. It hasn't been that long."

"But you haven't been wooing or been wooed, Maggie, and ergo, I am all ears."

Oh, crud. "No, no, that's not what I meant. Exactly the opposite of what I meant, in fact. I'm not in the market. And I need some advice."

"Oh. That's no fun."

Jackson snorted as if to agree.

Good grief. She was getting ganged up on, here.

"I need to make sure I'm not giving off the wrong impression," she said. "I offered to bring takeout for Asher tonight, and now that it's in my car, I'm paranoid that it telegraphs interest."

"I *knew* you were talking about Asher."

She turned her truck onto her street. "How? You've been in a baby haze."

"Lachlan and I do communicate with each other still," Marisol teased. "He said he thought there was something going on with Captain Librarian."

Maggie's stomach fluttered. Asher had more of

an undersea-superhero look going on rather than the patriotic, WWII-era variety, but Marisol wasn't totally off base with the description. Those arms definitely looked capable of ripping a chunk of firewood in two à la her favorite Chris Evans GIF... And there she went giving herself the wrong impression. She wasn't bringing Asher dinner because he was hot as sin. She was just trying to be kind. And to assuage her guilt for having turned down his friendly invitation the other night.

"There's nothing going on, nor do I want there to be," Maggie insisted. "Do you think I'm making a big mistake by bringing him dinner?"

"Did you use the word 'date' when you offered?"

"No. I didn't call it anything."

"Then I think you're safe." Amusement danced in Marisol's voice. "But if you *wanted* to call it something, you could think of worse—"

"Do you want me to rescind my babysitting offer?"

"You would never," Marisol said, still sounding overly entertained.

"I wouldn't." She pulled into her driveway and threw the vehicle in Park. "Nor would I date Asher."

She knew he wasn't like her ex-boyfriend Jeff. Asher wouldn't walk out with no warning or steal from her. But there were just too many ways for a relationship to go wrong.

A few minutes later, she walked into the main area of the addition and almost tripped over thin air.

He had the frame up for the shelving unit that spanned the length of one side of the room, and she'd caught him stretching to drill a hole in the frame.

Oh. My.

His faded blue T-shirt was a little damp between his shoulder blades. It molded to every back muscle, of which he had more than his fair share. And the baseball cap, backward on his head, and faded jeans cupping his perfect rear...

Maybe dinner could wait.

"Hey," she said, giving herself a shake. In no world would it be appropriate to consider something casual with Asher. He was a parent, and his brother was marrying one of Maggie's best friends.

But as he turned, his slow, easy smile made her belly all warm and needy... Would it really be that awkward to hook up with him?

Yeah, genius, it would. You really want to spend the next few decades running into him at Garnet's house, or the grocery store?

She smiled back and held up the bag of takeout. "Dinner has arrived."

He put a hand to his flat stomach. "Just in time. I'm starving. Want to hold this cabinet door for me, though? I want to get one up, see how it looks."

"Sure." She plunked the bag on a stack of floorboards and scanned the ground for hazards before unclipping Jackson from his leash.

"Not on the job tonight?" Asher asked, pointing the drill in his hand at the dog.

"I should probably be running him through another one of Marisol's exercises, but given the first eight didn't work…"

Jackson leaned against Asher and looked up at him with adoring eyes. Asher scrubbed him between the ears with a splayed hand. "You've got this figured out, don't you, big guy?"

"Well, we'll assume he does until Friday, at least." She strolled over, trying not to get too close before it was absolutely necessary. "What do you need me for?"

He lifted one of the pine-fronted doors into place. "Hold this just so, and I'll deal with the screws."

Do not think of double entendres. Do not.

Her hands shook a little and she pressed them against the wood to cover up the effect he had on her.

He smelled the best, really. Like a warm, clean man who knew how to use fabric softener and spent time around books. His right biceps flirted in the corner of her vision, flexing as he lifted the drill and slotted the bit into the screw.

The tool whirred and thunked three times. Jackson, who'd curled up in the corner, whimpered.

"You're okay, buddy," she called, trying to keep her gaze on the pale wood of the cabinet. But the sleeve of Asher's T-shirt hugging his upper arm was way too fascinating.

He inserted six more screws in quick succession before lowering the drill. "You can let go."

"Oh, right." Dropping her hands, she tore her gaze from his biceps and made eye contact.

Humor danced in his brown irises. His lips twitched. "Problem?"

Yes. Everything to do with you. "You're pretty fast at that."

He stilled, expression turning close to what Jackson's had looked like the one time she'd caught him snitching something off the counter.

Okay, what was that all about?

"You look guilty," she accused.

He covered his flash of culpability with a smile. "We're just hanging cupboard doors."

But the fact I want you to carry me over to the sawhorse and see how much weight it can hold... "I know we are."

"I know that, too," he replied seriously.

"Good."

And there was that crinkle of contrition again, screwing up one side of his face. "But I have a confession to make, Maggie."

She swallowed.

"I didn't need your help just now."

Gah, why was her mouth so dry? "No?"

He shook his head slowly. "I just wanted an excuse to be close to you."

"Oh…" She breathed out the exclamation.

"I know you're not looking for that, so I'd apologize, but I can't seem to…" Lifting his hand, the one not holding the drill, he brushed her cheek with rough fingertips. His skin smelled of wood shavings and a hint of metal. She inhaled a little deeper, resisting the urge to tilt her head into the caress.

"Don't. Apologize, that is," she added, before he could misunderstand and take his hand away. She couldn't stop herself from spreading her fingers wide on his chest, finally confirming for herself that his pecs were perfection. Heat seeped through the cotton, warming her palm. She missed this, the raw sensation of touching another human. But why this particular person? Why someone with so many strings and complications?

"What about…" He tilted his head down, a suggestion that he'd be good with getting even closer, but the foot separating them in height meant she'd need to meet him halfway.

Did she want to? Maybe just once. Just enough to learn how he tasted.

Once couldn't hurt.

Looping her arms around his neck, she rose on her toes and met his parted lips with hers.

He kissed softly, but with the promise of more. A

clear signal he'd let her lead, but as soon as she re-linquished control, he'd happily take over.

Oh. Oh, dear.

But she couldn't bring herself to pull away. He splayed a hand on her lower back, helping her stay on her toes, and wrapped the other arm around her shoulders. The cold plastic of the drill rested against her shoulder.

Good grief, Asher Matsuda's kissing eclipsed his ability to lay flooring or recite the Dewey decimal system. A woman could get lost in these arms, with his lips claiming and caressing…

A furry snout jammed itself in the seam of their bodies and let out a snuffle.

"Jackson!" she scolded, stumbling backward. The dog sidestepped into position, at the ready to stabi-lize.

Asher chuckled and rubbed a hand along his lips, looking a little dazed.

She drew a shaky breath and rested her hand on the dog. And she almost needed the support. Her knees had pretty much forgotten their main func-tion was to hold her body up.

"Well," she said lamely.

"Well."

"That was—" *Hot. Addictive.*

Stupid.

"Nice?" he offered.

Talk about an understatement. "Sure. And kinda

ill-advised, but—" she lifted a shoulder "—now we know."

"What, exactly, do we know?"

"That—"

That I want to do it again. The truth pushed to the surface, threatening to spill out.

No way could she admit that. It would be entirely unfair to give him the wrong impression. Heck, kissing had done that enough in the first place.

"You've been clear on not wanting to date, Maggie." He squeezed the back of his neck. "Dating's tricky for me, too. I don't know if Ruth is ready to see me moving on."

"Oh, of course." Selfish of her, not to be considering it from that perspective.

He brushed her cheek again, a slow stroke of his thumb that would be oh so good in all sorts of other places on her body.

She let out a noise of complaint, of lost possibilities.

The corner of his mouth turned up. "Doesn't mean I don't wish it could be otherwise, though."

She backed up a couple of steps. Even wishing seemed too much, too close to trying to figure out how it could be otherwise. Which was ridiculous— between her parents and Jeff, she'd learned long ago there was no point in figuring out love.

She shivered and wrapped her arms around herself. "I should go."

Jamming his hands in the back pockets of his jeans, he sent her a puzzled look. "Maggie, the food."

"You—you eat it," she stuttered, taking Jackson's leash out of the purse still slung across her body. She clipped the fastener to his collar. "Enjoy. Best pad Thai in town. Uh, only pad Thai in town. Fortunately, it's delicious." She was rambling. Awesome. "Better if I don't stay, though. I'll—I'll figure something out. Something else. For, uh, dinner."

His confused gaze bore into her back as she rushed from the building. Figuring out what to eat for dinner was the least of her worries. More importantly, she had to find a way to stop craving more of Asher Matsuda's kisses.

It only took five minutes of Lachlan running Jackson through his paces on Friday afternoon for Maggie's stomach to wobble. The observation session was relaxed, but precise. Her brother knew his stuff when it came to training dogs, and in the absence of any official state licensing, she trusted Lachlan was the best there was to evaluate an animal's progress. She wanted a second opinion to take back to the support animal organization.

"He's doing fine, Maggie," her brother assured her after Jackson successfully followed protocol in a staged collapse. "He's got that down pat."

"Yeah, because it's quiet back here."

"We'll head out somewhere busier in a bit. For

now, take him toward the opposite corner, pretend to lose your balance and not to revive," Lachlan instructed, examining with a sharp gaze.

She did, making sure to fall pell-mell. Jackson sprang into action, nudging her to try to rouse her. When she didn't, he barked. He was like a dog with a checklist: bark, run to Lachlan, bark again, accept praise from Lachlan.

"He's seamless," Lachlan pronounced as he knelt to give Maggie a hand up. "You've done great work with him."

"I know, but—"

A car horn rent the air from somewhere in front of the house.

Jackson yelped and skittered to the side.

"Marisol?" she asked, gut full-on plummeting.

Lachlan jerked his head in a short nod. "I asked her to surprise us so we wouldn't know when it was coming."

"I'd really hoped…" She sighed, resigned to the truth. "We can't risk him startling when he's in the middle of a physical assist."

Sympathy crossed Lachlan's face and he raked a hand through his tawny hair. "You did what you could, Maggie."

"I know. But now I have to say goodbye to Jackson *and* deal with not having trained him properly."

She wasn't feeling any better about that a couple of hours later as she walked the dirt trail around

Moosehorn Lake. After sending Lachlan and Marisol off to dinner with strict instructions to take at least two hours for themselves, she'd filled her truck with baby gear and brought her niece to the water. A vain attempt at sloughing off her bad mood.

Laura was a comforting weight in the baby sling on Maggie's chest, counteracting how Jackson's leash weighed her hand down as if it was made of lead, not nylon. Was he going to be unhappy without an official job? Would he be too bored?

She couldn't put off contacting the Parkinson's assistance organization she'd been working with any longer, though. Wanting to get it over with, she called her contact and explained the problems with Jackson's assessment.

"He's a career-change dog after all, is he?" Tom sounded calm but resigned.

"I'm so sorry, Tom. I tried everything I could, consulted with a canine psychologist, even, but when I had my brother run Jacks through his test today… He shakes, still. Jumps when he's startled. I can't break him of it. I mean, I have two weeks until I take on my next dog. I could keep trying, if you like. He's such a sweetheart. I might be able to make a breakthrough."

Her footsteps crunched on the path for a few seconds before Tom responded.

"No, I think we've exhausted all options," he said.

"We'll have to arrange for pickup. He'll be easy to rehome, at least."

"I know." Her stomach churned with guilt. Failing would sting for a long while.

And having to let Jackson go was even worse. She'd consider adopting him herself, but she had a new dog lined up to train in two weeks. It wouldn't be fair to the big goofball to have to divide her attention.

"I got attached to him more than my previous trainees," she admitted. "He's lovely. I wish he could be what you needed him to be."

"He'll be exactly what the people who adopt him needs him to be—a loving animal."

They arranged for Maggie to drive to Missoula to drop him off on Sunday and then hung up.

Laura let out a little baby squeak and nuzzled her face against the inside of the baby sling.

Jackson, ever alert to people noises, turned his head and gave the infant side-eye.

"What's that look for? You don't like human puppies?"

He grumbled an ah-roo.

"Oh, stop it. She's not mine." *And neither are you, big guy.* "I'm sorry, Jacks." She made him heel so she could scratch him between the ears, and her heart twisted. "Sorry I couldn't teach you what you need to know. And sorry I can't adopt you myself. But I have a new puppy coming."

His long tail drooped. He couldn't understand her words, but he definitely picked up on her tone.

Ten minutes later, they approached the end of the trail, near where an access path connected to a street dominated by a handful of houses with views of the lake. Garnet lived out here now, had moved from her place in town in order to get more time with Caleb, given how busy their schedules were. It was a modern monstrosity of a house, and Garnet was having fun softening the edges of the decor. If Maggie was in a better mood, she'd drop in and say hi, share some tea and commiserate. She wasn't suitable company for anyone older than two months, though.

"Sorry, Laura, you're stuck with Auntie Eeyore tonight."

Voices carried from down the path, interrupting her solitude. A group of people emerged from behind the wall of fir and pine trees, and a familiar, dark brown head came tearing down the trail, followed by her equally familiar father and his brother and sister-in-law-to-be. Good grief, had she summoned them or something?

Garnet and Caleb studied Maggie with enough interest that suspicion crept into her chest. What had Asher told them? Had he mentioned their ill-advised kiss?

"Jackson!" Ruth held out her arms.

"Ruth," Asher said, smiling at Maggie as he followed in his daughter's wake. "Check to see if he's working."

Regret tightened Maggie's belly. "You're free to fuss, Ruth."

The girl wasted no time, throwing her arms around Jackson's neck. Her family caught up a few seconds later.

Garnet, red hair bound in a messy bun and wearing a casual dress, immediately homed in on the baby, crowding in to Maggie's side to get a better look. "Ohhh, Maggie, look at that *face*." She crossed her hands over her breastbone. "Oh my God, I want one so much. Cale, we should really—"

"We should." Asher's brother's dark eyes twinkled, reflecting his bemused, contented smile. He looked a whole lot like Asher, minus the beard and a couple of inches in height. And even though Caleb was fit, he didn't look ready to walk into a superhero casting room.

Her fingers still held the sense memory of how hard Asher's chest had been. She tossed him a glance. "Hey."

He nodded his greeting, mouth twitching at the corner.

Could he tell what she was thinking about?

Ignore it. Moving along...

She refocused on Garnet. By the happy expressions she was sharing with the man she loved, Maggie was going to have more infants than just Laura in her life sooner rather than later. She sucked in a breath. How did the people in her life manage to barrel ahead with each other, ignoring how things could go so wrong? Believing that they'd be the ones to beat the odds?

And how do I get off, doubting their love and marring the beauty they've found, that they're continuing to create?

Sighing, she dropped a kiss on her niece's hat-covered head and held the leash out to Ruth. "Want to be in charge?"

Ruth nodded and happily took over, bounding down the trail with the dog.

Hands free, Maggie gave Garnet a side hug. "Margaret makes for an excellent middle name, you know. Or Reid, for a boy."

Garnet nudged her with an elbow. "Noted. I'll let Caleb know they're on the list."

Caleb came up and absorbed his fiancée into an embrace. "Tell me more about this list." Linking hands, they set off down the trail after Ruth.

Asher hung back, observing the scene with his arms loosely crossed. The affection on his face matched what Maggie felt whenever she managed to get together with her siblings.

"You have a pretty great family," she said. "Out for a walk?"

"Just waiting for dinner to finish cooking," he

explained. "I convinced Caleb to make our mom's lamb recipe."

She tried not to make a face. "I'm sure it's—" She shook her head. "Sorry. Can't pretend that sounds good."

He chuckled. "I get it. The thought of eating shrimp makes me gag. We all have our limits." He pointed to his family. "My daughter's annexed your dog—are you okay with changing direction?"

"Sure." Her earlier malaise settled over her again. "I'm looking for a distraction. Not picky about what kind."

Cocking an eyebrow, he set off in the same direction as his family, the one she'd come from. Didn't seem in a hurry to catch up to the group, though. Nor was she. Partly because she didn't want to inflict her mood on Garnet and Caleb, and partly because she loved having Asher, looking all cozy in a thick sweater and down vest, all to herself. She could see borrowing that sweater, wearing it on a day she had nothing better to do than snuggle up against his hard body and binge the latest Netflix series. It would smell like him, that mix of fresh air and fabric softener.

"Why a distraction?" he asked.

Because neither dwelling on Jackson or dreaming of lazy afternoons with you will have any positive results. "Lachlan tested Jackson today. He didn't pass. I have to take him back to the Parkinson's organization." She sucked in a breath. Ugh, it was feeling like Cleo all over again. Which was stupid, because she'd trained dogs before without getting this attached.

He rubbed her shoulder over the strap of the baby carrier. The comforting gesture eased her disappointment more than she wanted to admit.

She sighed. "I don't know why I got my hopes up so much. I knew there were no guarantees, given his anxiety."

"He's a special dog." He stared down the path, gazed fixed on his daughter as she let Jackson drag her to and fro. "Ruth will be sad to see him go."

"So will I," she admitted. "It's reminding me of when my ex moved and took—"

Ruth let out a yelp as Jackson broke free and bounded toward Maggie.

"Oh, crud. He shouldn't have done that." She snapped out a command and gave him a hand signal, and he galloped to her side. She took his leash and made him sit before they started walking again.

"Sorry, Maggie." Ruth ducked her head as they caught up to her. "I didn't mean to let go, but he yanked when he heard something in the bushes."

"He's strong. It'll happen."

"He's still learning, right? And soon you'll have him trained?"

Maggie's heart crashed to the dirt trail. "About that, Ruth—Jackson failed his testing today. He's going to be put up for adoption. He'll be placed in a really good home."

Ruth stopped so fast it kicked up dirt.

Maggie stumbled to avoid running into the girl, and the baby squawked in protest. One big hand gripped her shoulder and the other tenderly cupped Laura's back, steadying and stabilizing.

"You can't just stop like that, Ruthie." His tone was calm but firm.

"But, Daddy." Ruth knelt and hugged Jackson's neck. "He can't leave!"

Asher grimaced. He was still rubbing both the baby and Maggie's shoulder, and it was really hard not to scoot closer, steal a hug or a kiss or—

"He was always going to leave, peanut."

"We could adopt him!" Ruth cried, brown eyes glistening.

"We're not in a place to adopt a dog." Asher's jaw tightened. "We're still getting settled."

"I know. And Jackson's the best part of being here!"

Doubt crossed his face. "We'll talk about this later, okay?"

"But—"

"Later." He cut off the protest with an admirable mix of empathy and firmness.

Fisting her hands, Ruth spun and speed walked after her uncle and Garnet, who were strolling ahead, seemingly unaware of the family drama.

"This'll be fun," Asher said sarcastically, dropping his hands. The loss of contact echoed through her body. Laura didn't seem any happier with the change, squawking and squirming.

Maggie bobbed on her toes to settle the baby. "Sorry. I feel this is my fault, introducing Ruth and Jackson in the first place."

"Don't. It is what it is. I'm just frustrated that I keep having to say no to her."

Saying no was necessary sometimes, though. Setting limits to keep kids safe. And to keep her heart safe…

"Dogs are a lot of work," she said sympathetically.

"Alex and I both grew up with dogs," he mumbled. His jaw sagged, a flash of sadness that had to be bone deep.

"Lucky. My parents never had time for pets. I learned to love them when we moved in with my grandparents during the summers." *I learned to love, period. Not well enough, though.* Jeff had left her easily enough. "Jackson is crate trained. He can be by himself for parts of the day. Not that that would change things for you," she finished in a rush.

He lifted the corner of his mouth, a weak attempt at a smile, and the urge to step into him shimmered along her limbs. If only she could coax some happiness from him with her lips.

"Want to come to dinner tonight?" he said. "I'm sure there are enough options without the lamb, and

Ruth loves to have an audience when she practices Shabbat blessings."

She motioned to the baby and the dog. "I need to take Laura back to sleep in her bed. But thanks for the invite."

"Maybe one of these days I need to get the message, stop asking."

"No! That's not what it is." She laid a hand on his shoulder. "You're great. But I—"

"It's not you, it's me, Maggie?" He managed to look both amused and sad. "Been a while since I heard that one."

"It's true, though."

"Sort of. But I think you're selling yourself short."

She rocked back on her heels. "What does that mean?"

"Sit down with me for dinner sometime and I'll explain. Just as friends. I promise. I'm not looking for a relationship any more than you are." And he jogged off before she could get more of an answer.

Chapter Six

Ruth's ability to keep a good sulk going was down-right impressive. She alternated between pouting and sniffling all the way through dinner. Had it not been for the brimming tears, Asher would have gotten annoyed after the first hour, but she was genuinely sad. And he didn't need a reminder as to why the loss hit her extra hard.

She slunk over to the couch and buried her nose in a book after helping clear the table, leaving Asher standing in his brother's open-plan kitchen with a stack of dirty dishes and no damned clue what to do.

Caleb hitched a hip on the counter. "So Ruth wants a puppy."

"So Garnet wants a baby," Asher retorted, bending over to load the dishwasher.

His brother snorted. "And she'll get one, too. Something tells me Ruth won't be so lucky."

"She wants a Great Dane, Cale," he said as he started loading the dishwasher. "Not exactly, as you called him, a puppy."

"Does your lease allow animals?"

"Yes." But his bank account didn't. An adoption fee, not to mention the monthly kibble bill… It stung too much to admit that to his older brother, though. Both Caleb and Asher's twin, David, made exponentially more than Asher, given they both had "Dr." attached to their names.

Which made him question his life choices when it came to not being able to make Ruth happy.

Kids need love and structure, Asher, not money.

His mother's voice. Backed up by Alex on more than one occasion.

But in this moment, to Ruth, "love" and "Jackson" were the exact same thing.

"I'd make it work if I could," he said to his brother. "But this skiing gambit she's on—"

"I don't need to ski." A small, desperate voice came from behind him.

He put the last plate in the bottom rack of the dishwasher and straightened, turning toward his daughter. He caught his brother's retreating footsteps behind him, and the sound of the back porch door closing soon after.

Ruth's voice wasn't the only desperate part of her. Her dark eyes swam with sadness and a fraction of hope. Damn it, how was he going to live with himself if he extinguished that hope?

"What do you mean, you don't need to ski? It's all you've talked about these past weeks." In between facts about Great Danes, that was.

"If I don't join the ski team, I could take Jackson for walks every day, and—"

He held up a hand. "It's not just the time. It's… Dogs are expensive. And I'm good with the extra work I'm doing for the Reids on a short-term basis, to save up for equipment and a pass and club fees. But only short-term. It cuts too much into our family time."

"We don't have a family! Not a whole one!" She burst into tears.

"Oh, honey." He rushed to scoop her into an embrace, kneeling on the floor so he could hold her on his lap. Her body shook. And he tried to be strong for his daughter, to hold in his own sorrow. But it leaked out of him, stinging his eyes and thickening in his throat.

Alex, I could really use a hand right now.

He squeezed his eyes shut and pictured his husband's face, the humor that had danced on his mouth right until the end. *How about a paw?*

Yeah, that sounded like Alex, all right. As did throwing financial caution to the wind. For all his strengths, his husband had been an abysmal budgeter.

But you're the opposite.

He swallowed. Budgeting was one thing. Wizardry was another.

Footsteps shuffled behind him. Tightening his grip on Ruth, he turned his head. Both his brother and Garnet stood a few feet away. Caleb held a small notepad. He flashed it at Asher, angling it so that it was out of Ruth's line of sight.

If you can swing the ongoing costs, I'm happy
to cover the adoption fee and the pet insurance.

Oh great. His brother had overheard the message about money after all. Which… He locked gazes with Caleb. All he saw there was generosity and love. No judgment.

Yeah. Taking some money from his brother in order to make Ruth happy wasn't an issue at all. No point in holding on to his pride and harming his daughter in the process.

I owe you, he mouthed.

"Never," Caleb replied. "I love you. Both of you."

Garnet wiped at her eyes with the back of her hand and held out a Kleenex box.

He took it and nestled a tissue into Ruth's hand before nudging her chin with a finger.

"Let me give Maggie a call."

"About what?" she asked.

"We'll talk about it after." He didn't want to get her hopes up if this didn't work.

"Are you calling her about Jackson?" Ruth's voice rose to a gleeful squeak.

"Ruth, come see the stars. They're really bright tonight," Caleb said. Giving her a hand up from the floor, he guided her toward the back porch. Garnet trailed behind them.

Asher didn't bother moving to somewhere more comfortable. He leaned against one of the cupboards, stretched out his legs and took out his cell.

It rang four times before Maggie picked up.

"Hello?" An infant wail drowned out her greeting.

"Uh—oh," he said. "That doesn't sound good."

"I'm out of my element, here. She's had a bottle and a burp. She's swaddled and is in her bed… I'm rubbing her back, but she doesn't want to settle. Marisol says they never have to rock her to sleep, but…"

"Do what you need to do, Maggie. If she wants a snuggle, she wants a snuggle."

"I don't want to screw up the routine Lachlan and Marisol have set."

Asher smiled. "Babies love messing with routines."

"Fine. Give me a minute."

He waited, listening as both Maggie's shushing and the infant's cries grew distant, then lessened.

"Hey," she whispered. "We're in the rocking chair. Seems to be working."

"Solid choice." As much as he'd give anything to have Ruth be tiny again, just for a few hours, he did not miss the sleepless nights and purple crying jags. "Sorry to catch you at a bad time. I thought you'd be home by now."

"Marisol and Lachlan decided to go to a movie after dinner. They need this. Date night is really important."

So how come they can have love and a family, but you can't? The question rested on his tongue, but that was something to ask when they weren't on the phone.

"Do you think we'd be eligible to adopt Jackson?"

For a moment, all he heard were the baby's slowing whimpers. "I didn't think you wanted to take him on."

"I was worried about the finances. But that—well, we figured that out. I think he'll be good for Ruth."

"I do, too." Her concern softened into joy. "Let me talk to my contact tomorrow. I love the idea of Jackson staying in Sutter Creek where I can see him."

And he loved the guarantee that he'd keep seeing her after he finished the renovations.

* * *

"That bed would fit me."

"And Ruth would fit in the food bag." Maggie couldn't help but laugh at Asher's stunned expression as he took in the pile of Jackson detritus crowding her front entryway on Monday afternoon. God, his dropped jaw was adorable. Not to mention the way his cardigan hugged his shoulders...

That's sexy, not adorable.

Ack, she really needed to stop noticing that.

"How was the drive to Missoula?" She'd organized things so that Asher and Ruth could spend their Sunday finalizing the adoption at the assistance dog organization. As soon as Maggie had gotten the confirmation that Asher's adoption offer was approved, she'd arranged for him to come pick the dog up from her house after work on Monday. And now Ruth and Jackson were outside, happily playing on her lawn. It was as if the pup knew he had a new family.

"We made good time. Ruth was so happy over the reason for the long drive that she didn't complain about not stopping. Beautiful view, regardless," he said. "Come the spring we'll have to do some exploring. I'd love to head south, show Ruth Old Faithful."

Maggie's heart panged. Family road trips hadn't been a thing for the Reids. When her parents hadn't been working at their Chicago law firm, they'd been busy freezing each other out, and using their children as chess pieces in the process. She had no doubt Asher would never treat Ruth like a pawn.

He probably wouldn't freeze a woman out, either.

"I—uh—" She cleared her throat, pushing away the unhelpful thought. "The prismatic spring is even more impressive. Living in the mountains and near the parks and backcountry is one of the reasons I settled here." She'd worked as a day trip guide for Sutter Mountain Resort while she was putting herself through college. Maybe she should offer to take him and Ruth to a few of her favorite places…

Her nerves jittered. She couldn't bring herself to force out the invitation. "You probably need to get going. Introduce Jackson to his new space."

He glanced over his shoulder out the screen door before fixing his gaze on her and running the pad of his thumb along her cheek. "Need to and want to don't seem to be lining up at the moment."

"What do you mean?"

"I do need to get home to cook dinner. But I'd rather keep standing here, staring at you. You've gotten under my skin, Maggie. Even though you don't want to be there."

"Depends on how you define 'under my skin.'" Going against every intelligent cell in her body, she took a step closer to him, close enough to trace a line along his open shirt collar. "If it's that I'm bothering you? That's no good. But if it's that you're thinking about me? Well, join the club."

He looped his hands around her ribs and bent to her ear. "'Thinking' doesn't quite encompass it, though."

"Oh," she said. She rested her forehead against his chest and settled her hands on his hips. She could seriously breathe in the smell of him for a good year and not get tired of it.

"Daddy?"

He stumbled back from the embrace, turning to face his daughter, who crossed her arms and eyed them with scientific intensity.

Maggie tried to look blasé. "We should get these supplies in the car for you."

Ruth frowned at Maggie.

Crud, was the girl going to ask why Maggie had been plastered against Asher? What could possibly be a good answer—?

"Jackson keeps running away," Ruth complained.

Relief washed through Maggie. The frown was dog related. "That's one of the ways a dog plays. And though he's well trained, he's been adult focused until now. And I'll tell you a secret—obedience training is more about training the person rather than the dog. You and I can practice some commands and body language while your dad's working on the cabinets on Wednesday, if you like." She turned her attention back to Asher. "I'd recommend the two of you take one of my brother's classes, but I know Jackson best."

"Works for us."

The pleasure warming his expression suggested he was only too happy that she'd committed to spending more time with them.

And the happiness in her heart wanted her to agree.

Later that evening, she was sitting on her couch, trying to convince herself she was fine.

But her house felt cavernous without Jackson to take up all the space. She couldn't sit at the breakfast bar in the kitchen without noticing his dishes were gone. The living room couch was no better—it seemed all wrong without his giant butt leaning against the edge.

Also, it was way too hard to avoid the truth when she was alone: it wasn't just Jackson she was wanting to spend her evening with. It was Asher and Ruth, too.

Thanks, but no thanks for the reminder, brain.

Throwing on workout clothes, she hopped in her truck and drove to the wellness center. Going to the gym wasn't always her thing, but sweating away her loneliness seemed healthier than digging into a pint of ice cream and numbing herself with Netflix. Plus, as gyms went, the one at Evolve Wellness was top-notch. She walked past the reception area, all glass and barn wood, and headed straight for a treadmill. Most of the machines were empty—not surprising. Who else didn't have anything to do after dinner on a Monday? A few people were participating in the spin session being held in the fitness classroom off the gym, and a familiar, willowy, white man was spotting a for a powerlifter, an equally familiar, bald, black man with the build of a running back.

She waved at her receptionist and his boyfriend. Once Deon put the bar down, they both grinned and waved back.

There. She wasn't the only one coming to the gym after dinner on a Monday... Except Evan and Deon, a physical therapist who worked out of Evolve's PT clinic, were here together. The pair spent any time where they weren't working either rock climbing or training for it. Something they shared.

I don't need together. *I need not to feel rejected.*

And the only way to guarantee not getting rejected was to avoid handing someone her heart.

Taking out her frustrations on the treadmill, she ran hard for about twenty minutes before a call interrupted the podcast she was listening to.

It was her sister. Concern jolted through her.

"Are you okay?" she answered, panting to catch her breath.

"Yeah. Why wouldn't I be? And I'm not the one who sounds like a wheezing pug."

"I do not. I was running."

Stella chuckled. "That explains it. Got a minute?"

"I guess." She wiped down the machine and went into the hallway outside the gym. "What's up?"

"I'm worried Lachlan is taking too much on, and by extension, so are you. If you're having to borrow more money, is everything really okay?"

The back of her neck prickled. If Stella had bothered to come home once in the last decade, she'd know Maggie had more business than she knew what to do with, and that Lachlan's addition would only enhance her existing business. But pointing that out would be a wasted effort. Stella was hardened against returning. Something Maggie could avoid by making sure she didn't get involved in a failed relationship. "You saw his business plan. It's solid."

"I just—" Stella paused, yawning audibly. "I worry about you guys."

"Lachlan's fine. He and Marisol are brimming with new parent joy." Maggie winced. Babies were a sore subject with her sister, after the miscarriage she'd gone through at eighteen.

"As they should be. Marisol seems good for Lachlan," Stella murmured. "And whenever I've Skyped with them, it's clear he's head over heels for Laura and more than ready to be a dad. I wish…"

Maggie leaned against the hallway wall, guessing at where her sister's mind had gone. "No one's ready right out of high school."

"Yeah, obviously."

Hope leapt in Maggie's chest. Getting the chance to even talk about Stella's feelings was progress. Maybe her sister was softening to the idea of letting her siblings in. "It's still a loss, Stella. And you can be happy for Lachlan and still hurt for yourself. There's no statute of limitations on grief."

Silence rang on the other end. "You're a vet, Maggie, not a psychologist. And how about you fix your own issues before you poke at mine?"

The quick shift from sad to prickly caught Maggie for a loop. "What do you mean, mine?"

"You haven't had a serious relationship since Jeff."

"Why would I, given how that ended?" she exclaimed. "And what happened to *promise me you'll never be as stupid as me, Maggie*?"

Stella made a choking sound. "You remember that?"

"How could I forget?" Stella's sobs that difficult day were imprinted on her brain.

"Maggie, I was eighteen with zero judgment. Not all men are Ryan, or Jeff for that matter. And working a fifteen-hour day only to come home to an empty house is lonely."

Maggie sucked in a breath. "I don't work fifteen-hour days."

"Yeah, you do."

Okay, well, between dog training, search and rescue, and work, she did. "Fine. But I'm not lonely." It was one thing feeling empty, but admitting it to her sister? No, thanks. "I have more friends and family to hang out with here than you do in New York."

"I— Ouch, Maggie. How do you know? You've never visited."

"Because you've never invited me." Longing gripped her chest. "We could change that, though."

Stella paused for a long time. Her voice was rough when she finally said, "Work is complicated right now. I have a lot—I can't—I'm sorry. Soon."

"Soon. Sure." And she hung up on her sister before Stella had the chance to change "soon" to "never."

Tuesday morning, Asher dropped Ruth off at school, where she proudly showed off her new dog to her friends. Then he took their giant buddy home while he went to work, promising to come let the dog out on his lunch break. Hopefully it would go well and Asher wouldn't have to hide Jackson in his office, breaking regulations. The dog had slept okay in his new home, but had definitely seemed out of sorts. Missing Maggie, no doubt.

Asher could relate.

He spent his morning putting together a Halloween-themed book display in the children's section and helping patrons. As the minutes ticked closer to lunch, he grew more worried about how Jackson was coping. Maybe Maggie would be able to ease his fears.

He pulled out his phone and sent a quick text.

Asher: Someone missed you last night.

His cell buzzed.

Maggie: I'm going to assume you mean J

He grinned to himself. He had, but it could apply to him, as well. And for whatever reason, he didn't mind her knowing that. It was weird, really. It seemed less than prudent to consider getting involved with someone, given Ruth was still grieving and adjusting to the move. It would be a while before he'd even consider broaching the idea of him dating. And Maggie had been very clear she wasn't interested in a relationship, ever.

But flirting a little… It was a welcome break from the usual grind of working and parenting and keeping a household together.

It was worth a try.

And if I wasn't? he replied, reaching for his mug of tea.

Maggie: Well, I wouldn't suggest sleeping with one of my T-shirts like I would for Jackson.

He almost spat his mouthful of Sticky Rice Oolong tea onto his cell phone. No, if there was ever a time sleeping and Maggie Reid crossed over in his life, he didn't suspect her T-shirt would be in play. Not after he took it off, anyway.

Man, it was tempting to reply with "what would you suggest I sleep with?" but he was feeling a little gun-shy. Before he could either gather up the courage for innuendo or come up with a completely innocent response, another message arrived.

Maggie: I'll bring something over for him.

Excitement coursed through him. Dropping something by, giving Ruth some lessons tomorrow—two visits in two days sounded just right.

Jackson would earn some extra dog biscuits if he kept luring in a certain veterinarian. The cookies might help get the dog out of his funk, too.

When Asher ran home to let him out, the canine was calm but morose. They had a good walk around the neighborhood before time ran out and Asher needed to go back to work. Jackson didn't seem anxious when Asher left, calming Asher's concerns somewhat.

He was sitting at one of the computer tables in the back corner of the library, helping one of the senior patrons with an internet query, when familiar footsteps caught his attention.

Maggie appeared from around a shelf, clutching a reusable shopping bag.

His heart lifted, and he smiled. Too obvious? A little pathetic? At least one of those things.

Probably both.

Cheeks pink, she scanned the scene and motioned to him that she'd wait.

Asher nodded, refocusing on the white-haired woman trying to fill out a form on a seniors' social website. "Does that make sense, Mrs. Brooks?"

"Absolutely, dear. I'd have asked my grandson to show me, but he just lost his wife, did you hear? He has bigger problems than helping his granny navigate the internet."

Asher hadn't heard about someone being widowed recently. A knot of sympathy filled his throat. He cleared it and screwed up his face in an expression he hoped fell between *I've been there* and *I'm sorry*.

"That's a terrible loss," he said quietly. "My husband died close to two years ago, and I can say for me that day-to-day distractions were necessary for getting out of bed. That, and my daughter."

"I'm so sorry you lost your love." She laid a thin-skinned hand on his forearm. "My grandson's children keep him plenty busy. But I don't think he needs to see me trying to find dates online right when he's in mourning."

Asher blinked and studied the site closer. Oh, geez. It *was* a dating site. He'd missed that the first time he'd glanced at it.

He shot her a half smile. "Fair point. But if there

are other ways you can keep him busy, give it a shot. He'll thank you. Eventually."

She patted his cheek. "You'll fit in just fine in Sutter Creek, Asher. Now go see what our pretty veterinarian has for you in that bag she was carrying."

"Oh, it's something for my dog."

Mrs. Brooks shook her head. "I don't believe that for a second." She shooed him away with a hand.

Dismissed, he strolled in the direction Maggie had gone. She wasn't by the desk or in the open area with the displays, so he poked his head down a few shelving rows until he spotted her blond head.

She was back in the true crime section, like she had been the first day he'd noticed her and Jackson. Was wearing scrubs again, too. Unsurprising, since she must have left work to come here. *She did it for the dog, not for me.*

But a man could dream. Some naive, romantic part of him, a part that had survived despite of—or perhaps because of—Alex, could easily imagine Maggie popping in to share lunch, or a secret kiss in the stacks… Nerves fluttered in his chest, and the corners of his mouth quirked up.

"It seems Jackson is missing his true love," he said.

Maggie's lips formed an *O*. "He was only with me for a few months."

"Apparently it only took that long to make an impression." He stepped closer and brushed a stray curl off her cheek. "I can see how that would happen."

"Asher..." Longing flickered across her face. She bit her lower lip.

He flexed his hands at his sides to keep from tracing his thumb along the pink flesh. "Yeah?"

"You're flirting with me." She said it softly, warily, as if she couldn't decide if she liked it or not.

"Yeah."

Her brow furrowed. "And you're at work."

"Is that the only reason you don't like it?"

Her chest rose with a deep breath. Her earlier flush returned to her cheeks. "Who said I didn't like it?"

"A hunch."

She glanced over her shoulder and around him before rising up to steal a kiss. "You clearly shouldn't listen to your hunches."

Clearly not. Sliding his fingers into her hair, he sank into the kiss. She tasted like mint, as if she'd anticipated this and popped a breath freshener.

His pulse kicked up. Drove higher as her hands skimmed his back.

She murmured a pleasure-filled sound that hummed along his skin.

A throat cleared behind him. "I have a book to check out when you get a second. Is that you there, Maggie?"

Maggie sprang back at Mrs. Brooks's question. "Oh, goodness. I'm so sorry."

"Don't let me interrupt." Amusement colored the older woman's tone. "What's a library for, if not a little romance? Those books are one aisle over, though, aren't they?"

"That's— It's not—" Maggie croaked, seemingly unable to finish a sentence. A deep red flush swept from her neck to her hairline.

Asher palmed his mouth, smoothing his beard and turning on his winningest smile. "Apologies, Mrs. Brooks. Let me check out your selection for you."

It took everything he had, not to kiss Maggie one more time before he went to his desk. But one stolen embrace was plenty for today.

Flirting was one thing. Making a habit of this woman was entirely another.

Chapter Seven

"I need to know everything."

Maggie froze, hands hovering over the tray she was preparing with kitten vaccinations. She'd thought she was alone in the treatment room, but the command coming from the doorway proved her wrong. And she didn't need to turn to confirm who'd spat out the command. She knew Emma Halloran's breathy alto almost as well as she knew her own voice, having been friends with the woman since they were preteens. Her stomach sank. Word about yesterday's kiss with Asher had clearly spread like wildfire.

She hadn't talked to him about it, had left the

bagged T-shirt at his desk and rushed out with a cursory goodbye while he was checking out Mrs. Brooks's novels. He'd texted her a pointed Very nice to see you.

She hadn't known how to reply beyond a You, too. And she had no idea what she'd say to him when she saw him this evening for Ruth's lesson.

She didn't face her friend, stayed focused on the tray. And readied herself to evade like a guerrilla army. "Hey, Em. Anything you want to know, I'm here for. Four months is a key age for cats, so I'm sure you have lots of questions."

"I'm not talking about Splotches."

Maggie turned slowly, raising an eyebrow.

Emma's insistent expression was at odds with how tenderly she cradled her sixteen-week-old calico kitten. Her chestnut hair was up in a ballerina bun—unlike Maggie's untamable mop, Emma's sleek strands wouldn't dare fall out of the just-so style. Emma wore a navy blue blazer over a white blouse and jeans. Her stiletto heels gave Maggie arch pain just looking at them.

"You must be spending a fortune in lint rollers if you're cuddling her in your work clothes," Maggie said mildly, waving Emma in and stroking the kitten under the chin as soon as she got close enough to reach.

"I'm quickly becoming the pet store's most frequent customer—" Emma cut herself off, straightening. She handed over the kitten and pinned Maggie down with a determined squint. "Stop getting me off topic! You were smooching in the library with that hottie librarian, and I had to find out from my mother, who heard from Mrs. Brooks?"

"Oh, hi there, precious," Maggie said to the cat, ignoring the question again. She was not talking about it, not even with her bestie.

"I know my intel is good, Maggie."

Her friend's confidence wasn't ill-placed. If anyone had their ear to the ground in Sutter Creek, it was Emma, who worked in marketing for her uncle's ski resort and had been tapped into the gossip supply chain since birth. The Hallorans were longtime residents, and Emma's parents managed a ranch that had been handed down through the generations. And by owning Sutter Mountain Resort, Emma's uncle essentially owned half the town.

Maggie trusted Emma. She really did. But she trusted her gut more. And her gut had always kept her safe.

Alone.

Exactly, safe. Maggie snuggled the young calico under her chin, taking a deep breath. Nothing centered her like animals did. But even Splotches's steady purring couldn't shake the jitters she'd been feeling since she kissed Asher yesterday.

"Let me take a look at you, Splotches." She started

examining the kitten, feeling to see if his adult teeth had started to come in and checking his ears and nose.

Emma flopped in the client chair against the wall next to the sink and glared at Maggie. "Can you look and dish at the same time?"

"Can and will are very different things, Em."

Emma growled.

"Oh, are you here for a well animal visit, too?"

"Maggie! Seriously."

Maggie paused her exam, placing the kitten on the table and holding it to stop it from scrambling away. "I'm being a thousand percent serious. In that I don't want to talk about it."

"Obviously. But why?"

Because I'm missing whatever quality it takes for people to stick around. And I'm not pulling a perfectly nice man and his daughter into my dysfunction.

Instead of confessing to that terrifying truth, she lifted a shoulder. "Because the kiss didn't mean anything."

"Liar. If it didn't mean anything, you wouldn't be putting on the secretive routine."

Oof. Nothing like a best friend to toss out truth bombs as if they were Halloween candy.

"Was it a crappy kiss?" Emma prodded.

"It was fine." Maggie palpated the kitten's abdomen. Her cheeks heated as the memory of pressing her lips to Asher's flooded her senses. His quiet control. Firm hands in her hair, thumb idly stroking her cheek. The hint of cologne on his skin. The hint of desire in his eye.

She'd be reliving those twenty seconds for years.

Taking a deep breath, she put on her stethoscope and listened to the cat's breathing.

A slow, satisfied smile stretched Emma's perfectly lipsticked mouth. "Thought so."

"Shh," Maggie said, pointing at her ear.

Emma waited patiently until Maggie removed her stethoscope. "Are you going to kiss him again? See him again? Go on a date? You should go on a date." She cocked her head in thought. "Oh! The harvest days out at the ranch. He's new to town, probably hasn't gone yet."

"He has a brother to play tour guide."

"But you're good at it."

Maggie sighed. "I'm seeing enough of him with the interior finishing he's doing on the expansion. Plus, I'm helping him with his dog. He adopted Jackson, in case you hadn't heard."

"I *had* heard. He's clearly perfect, Maggie, if he's able to take on that big galoot. And his daughter sounds like a sweetheart."

"She is. I'm giving her obedience lessons tonight."

Emma's smile grew contemplative. "Probably tough to fit in more kissing with his daughter around."

"There won't be more kissing." Asher deserved someone who matched his belief in love.

She swallowed. Picturing Asher embracing any-one else in the nonfiction section made her stomach lurch. Jealousy and nausea came in the same shade of green, apparently.

Maggie picked up the kitten and nuzzled his scruff. Splotches was her last appointment of the day, so she didn't need to hurry. Not with the cat, anyway. With her friend, she needed to give some sort of diversionary answer. Emma clearly wasn't going to back down without some solid reasoning.

"Even if I was wanting to date someone, which I'm not, I wouldn't get involved with a guy who has a kid, Emma. Especially not one who's still grieving."

Emma frowned. "Do you think he's not ready to start seeing someone?"

"I have no idea. But either way, I can't give him and his daughter the kind of stability they need."

"Can't and won't are two very different things, Maggie," Emma said, throwing Maggie's earlier claim back in her face. "I wouldn't shove you in just anyone's direction, you know." She crossed her arms. "You gotta have high standards. But the other day I went into the library to get a few books I had on hold, and I can say—definitively—that I will never look at barcode scanning the same way again. His *hands*, Maggie—"

Footsteps echoed in the hall and Maggie waved with one hand, cutting Emma off.

"Shh! Do you want Evan to hear?" Being disgustingly in love, Maggie's receptionist had capital-*O* opinions on her love life. Mainly that she needed one.

And Evan was usually right about most things— the guy was whip smart and kept her life organized down to the fourth decimal point—but he was way off when it came to this.

"Would getting Evan on my side change your mind?" Emma asked.

"No."

"I just want you to be happy, Maggie."

"Partnering up isn't the universal answer to happiness, you know."

The corners of Emma's mouth turned down, but she didn't disagree.

A couple of hours later, Maggie had finished up with Splotches's checkup, eaten dinner and obsessed about what to wear for Ruth's lesson for a good half hour before heading around back of the clinic to the expansion. Man, it was weird not having a blue-gray shadow.

Said blue-gray shadow bounded over to her two seconds after she opened the main door to the training barn. He jammed his nose against her rib cage and snorted, eyes pleading.

"Oh, don't give me that face, sir. I know for a fact Asher fed you today. And came home for lunch, and then I bet Ruth's been dishing out all sorts of love since school let out." Even so, she dropped to her knees and let Jackson flop in her lap. Well, his head and shoulders, anyway. His front legs stuck out like umbrella spokes and his back half sprawled on the floor.

Ruth raced over wearing pigtail braids, a unicorn T-shirt and an eager expression. "We've been playing fetch down the hallway. He doesn't always come back when I call him, though."

Rhythmic hammering, coming from Lachlan's future office, punctuated Ruth's words. Asher was hard at work, then. And not in the main area, where, now that it was cleaned of any construction mess, Maggie planned to work with Ruth and the dog. Well, being in different rooms would make it easier to focus. Since yesterday's kiss, her fingers had become mighty interested in walking their way up Asher's back again. Which wouldn't be happening again, and definitely wasn't an appropriate thing to focus on while teaching his daughter how to properly issue canine commands.

"Tell you what." Jackson lifted his head and looked at her expectantly. "No, goofball, not you." She focused on Ruth. "If you let your dad know I'm here, I'll get set up. And we'll start with basic behavior. Sit, lie down, come. It's a lot about tone. By the end of the evening, I bet you'll have it figured out."

Thankfully, Ruth didn't pick up on how Maggie was using her as a messenger, one hundred percent a chicken move. Asher didn't come out to greet her, either.

She should have been happy about that. But part of her wanted to go sulk in the corner.

Gah. Ridiculous. Both that she wanted his attention, and that she'd think he'd take the initiative when it was so obvious she was trying to avoid him.

I'm not here for Asher. I'm here for Ruth.

She kept reminding herself of that over the next forty-five minutes whenever her thoughts shifted to the man continuing to hammer, drill and saw in the other room. The noise was constant enough that it didn't seem to bother Jackson too much. He jumped on occasion, but didn't whine. Maybe her efforts from the past month hadn't gone to as much waste as she'd thought.

She worked on building Ruth's confidence and assertiveness until it was clear the girl was starting to run out of steam.

"Done for tonight?" Maggie asked. "You've got the three commands down, I think." She could see why Lachlan liked teaching so much. Remembering Ruth's smile from the end of the lesson when she had given an order and how Jackson had snapped to attention, sat his butt on the ground and then lay down, would keep Maggie going for a while.

Jackson flopped to his side and harrumphed.

Ruth joined him, using his rib cage as a pillow. "I kinda want to read my book," she admitted, expression sheepish. "Sorry."

"Oh, geez, never apologize for that." Maggie nodded at the dog. "He loves to be read to, if you want to give it a go."

Actually, she should suggest that to Asher. Jackson's anxiety prevented him from being physically reliable enough for someone with Parkinson's, but maybe she could keep training him for a different job. He was so sweet around kids—he'd probably love a reading support job. The school and library programs that used dogs to increase literacy were fascinating, and with how much Asher prioritized children's literacy, she could see Asher being on board with adding a dog to the library repertoire, especially if it meant he got to take Jackson to work sometimes.

Ruth scrambled to get her book, then resumed her lounging with her nose buried in the novel, a dog-eared copy of *Harry Potter and the Half-Blood Prince*.

"That looks well loved," Maggie commented, heart warming at the smile on the girl's face.

"Yeah, Dad read it to me already." Ruth glanced away from the pages to study Maggie. "What house are you in?"

"Ravenclaw, I think." She wasn't a plotter like a Slytherin.

And not nearly brave enough to be a Gryffindor.

That voice sounded suspiciously like Emma's.

"I'm Ravenclaw, too," Ruth said. "And I think Jackson's a Hufflepuff."

Maggie smiled. Man, she loved Ruth's creativity. Getting to parent such a fantastic girl would be rewarding as anything. Startled by the thought, she cleared her throat. "Oh, for sure. That would make a good Halloween costume for him."

Ruth nodded, gaze flicking back to Hogwarts and magic.

Time to say a quick goodbye to Asher and be on her way.

She hurried to the office and lurked in the doorway for a few seconds. Asher with power tools continued to provide a heck of a view. Warmth spread through her limbs as she watched his back muscles flex. Yep, those were the ones her fingers wanted to explore again.

As soon as he set down the saw, she called out, "Hey. I'm on my way out."

He turned, taking off the safety goggles he was wearing over the navy plastic frames that made his face just that much more alluring. The goggles dangled from one of his fingers. Yeah, Emma had been so right about his hands...

"Uh, Maggie?" he asked, curiosity flickering in his dark eyes. "Everything okay?"

"Sure." Mouth dry, she swallowed. "Lesson went well. We've established that the dog is a Hufflepuff."

Asher laughed. "Of course you did. Are you a Potterhead?"

"I'll admit to that." She crossed her arms. "I have an idea. What would you think about me trying to train Jackson as a literacy support dog? It wouldn't be as involved as service dog training. I could fit it in, even once my new puppy arrives."

He came closer, leaned a shoulder on the door frame. He smelled like wood shavings and warm cotton. And given he was a little sweaty, his lips would probably be salty. Which sounded like something she needed to test out...

"Intriguing. I like it. Let me look into it." He brushed a strand of hair off her cheek.

"Uh, great."

"Maybe next time I'm here, Ruth won't be," he murmured in her ear.

She closed her eyes, trying to keep her breathing even. "And what would that accomplish?"

"Who knows?" He traced her jawline with a finger, making her shiver.

Opening her eyes, she forced a stern expression. "I know I gave you the wrong impression when I kissed you yesterday, and I'm so sorry that I opened you up to that, because now the whole freaking town is going to know what happened..."

He sobered. "I'd love to say it didn't matter, but being gossiped about doesn't always end well for me. And I have Ruth to think of."

"Right. Both important things to consider. Also, people might make assumptions that there's something going on between us."

A dark brown brow lifted. "Isn't there?"

She backed up against the other side of the doorframe. "There shouldn't be."

"But there is."

She locked eyes with him. "Seems so."

He nodded slowly. "How does that line up with you not wanting to be in a relationship? I mean, I'm not calling this a relationship—" he rushed to correct himself "—but it's definitely interest, maybe even involvement, and I kind of need specifics on where that starts and ends. I'm not ready to open Ruth up to me seeing someone yet."

Maggie's heart stuttered. Between envisioning Asher reading Harry Potter to his daughter in that low voice of his and seeing him putting Ruth's needs first, she was close to melting into a woman-shaped puddle on the newly laid floor. He did fatherhood right. Something completely foreign to her own experience. She used to yearn for that bond between father and daughter before she gave up on believing her dad loved her. If she was being honest with herself, she lacked that closeness in most of her relationships.

And yeah, being alone meant not getting hurt anymore.

But then, alone hurt in and of itself.

She studied Asher, not knowing how to respond to his need to categorize the feelings between them. "I—I don't want to get between you and Ruth. And being involved beyond a couple of spontaneous kisses—"

—sounds really tempting.

"Isn't what you want, I know."

But…was it? If Asher could be so good as a father, could he be a good partner, too? And if she took a step in that direction, would they be able to build that connection?

She'd never believed herself capable. And she didn't see how it could turn into a long-term thing. That would mean being a mother to Ruth, something she'd never seen herself as qualified to do. Her own sure hadn't provided any appropriate role modeling.

She buried her face in her hands. "This is all way too much, way too soon."

"What, kissing?" He sounded puzzled.

She slid her hands down so she could see his face. "Sort of."

Couldn't exactly admit that she'd gone from kissing to hypothesizing about parenting his daughter.

"I don't know how to be what you would need," she explained. "And even if I could, none of it's good for Ruth." She cupped his cheeks and pulled him down a little so she could kiss him. Could savor the roughness of his beard on her palms and his tongue tangling with hers and his taste flooding her senses.

Tearing away from him before her impulsiveness got them caught again, and this time by the one person who'd be hurt the most, she backed out of the doorway.

He reached up with one hand and braced himself on the upper frame. Rubbing his lips with his other hand, he let out a low, rumbling laugh. "I dunno, Maggie Reid. You're at least a little bit of what I need."

A little after nine on Saturday evening, Asher stood in Lachlan's office with his hands on his hips, glancing between the doorless cabinets and the shivering dog. Getting all the fronts installed, his goal for the night, was taking twice as long because he was using a manual screwdriver so as not to aggravate Jackson's sensitivities.

And the extra time in the office with only the dog for company was giving him way too much time to think. Ruth was off at her first sleepover since they moved to town, a clear sign she was making steps to adapt to life in Sutter Creek. So how would she feel about him making steps, too? Would she judge him?

Hell, should he be judging himself for feeling ready to explore life again?

Some days, it felt like Alex had been gone forever, and others, like it was only yesterday he'd stopped sitting shiva.

"You got any wisdom on dating as a widower, buddy?" he asked the dog.

Jackson harrumphed and sent him a put-upon look.

"I know. Life is so much harder when you're a Dane, isn't it?"

Chuckling at the dog's expressive face and quiet *ah-roo*, he returned to his task, managing to get four doors up without traumatizing the canine.

He was on the verge of starting door number five when a female voice called his name.

Startling, he spun toward the voice he'd been hearing in his dreams for weeks. His face heated at his reaction. "The dog's wearing off on me, it seems."

"Sorry for the shock." Maggie stood in the doorway of Lachlan's office, the last place he'd seen her.

The last place they'd kissed.

A good moment. His heart warmed, and he held himself back from striding over and reliving the taste of her lips.

Jackson had no such hesitation, scrambling across the floor to greet Maggie. She crouched and gave him a big hug and an obligatory "oh yes, you're the best boy," before standing and brushing off her sweater. It was pale pink and cozy looking and wrapped around her much like Asher would enjoy doing.

Unsure if she wanted that, he leaned against the door he'd just hung. "Hey, there. Didn't expect to see you."

She lifted a shoulder and clutched the two sides of her sweater together with one hand. "I got home from having dinner with a friend and saw the lights on."

"Not a burglar."

"I knew it was you." Her voice hinted at intent of some sort. But what kind? "You're here late. Where's Ruth?"

"Sleepover. And Jackson and I were just sitting at home, staring at each other after dinner, so I figured I'd be productive in some way. It was too late to make social plans."

"Is it?" She entered the office, skirting his saw-horse table.

He cocked a brow. "Maybe I was wrong."

But instead of coming directly to him, as she'd done the other day, she stopped a few feet away to examine the shelving. "Nice work."

"Up to standards, I hope," he said.

She ran a hand along the doors. "Looks level to me." She stepped closer and traced a line across his pecs with the back of her hand. She flushed, dropping her arm to her side. "I'm terrible at this."

Catching her hip lightly with his fingers, he drew her in, dropping a kiss at her temple. Her hair smelled of raspberries, and it took effort to lift his nose away. "I haven't hooked up with anyone new in over a decade, Maggie. If anyone's rusty, it's me."

"You just have to *exist* and it's a turn-on," she blurted, crossing her arms over her chest and turning even redder.

He chuckled. Alex had often complained that he was unfairly good-looking, but Asher had chalked that up to husband-bias. Besides, he wanted to be admired for how he treated people and for being a good father, not for his face. "You're good for the ego, Maggie Reid."

She squeezed her eyes shut. "Glad I could be of service."

Even though she looked uncomfortable as hell, she still wasn't backing away from him. That was something. He slid his palm around to the small of her back, nestling her closer to his side. Her sweater was as luscious as he'd predicted. "I'd planned on working for another hour or so, though if you had something else in mind…"

Her eyes blinked open. "I—uh—well—" She muttered something. *Fudge truffles* was his best guess. Then she cleared her throat. "I didn't come over to check on how much progress you'd made."

"No?"

Shaking her head, she said, "I was going to watch a movie, but my house was eerily empty."

"You want to borrow Jackson back?" he asked, unable to stop his cheek from twitching in amusement.

"No, I was hoping for *you*. But if you need to finish what you're doing…"

She had a point. The faster he completed the job, the sooner he could sign Ruth up for the ski team. But how many evenings would he get when he wasn't under a watchful, ten-year-old eye?

And how often would a kid-free night coincide with an invitation from Maggie that could potentially lead to snuggling with her some more, but on a couch instead of against a half-finished wall of cabinets?

"I really should keep working."

Her face fell. "Oh, I—"

"But I won't."

He kissed her. Just a quick brush. She let out another "oh," and he captured it with a deeper press. So much softness to take in: her lips. Her hair, tangled around his fingers. Her sweater, a thin barrier between his fingers and her skin. But underneath it, she wasn't all soft. He'd seen her strength at work, and her strength of conviction, too.

And he wanted to know more about her.

"Do you like extra butter on your popcorn?" he asked, breaking the kiss.

Her jaw dropped in clear faux offense. "I'm not a *monster*. And Jackson wouldn't speak to me if I tried to feed him plain popcorn."

"I knew he fit into my family for a reason."

"Which, given it's hard for him to fit anywhere..." she cracked.

They both looked over at the dog, who stared dolefully from his mat in the corner.

"Oh, I'm kidding, big guy," Maggie said. She glanced up at Asher, eyes bright with humor. "He'll probably insist on taking the couch. We'll be relegated to the floor."

He grinned. He didn't care where he sat, so long as he got the chance to be close to this woman. Though she wouldn't want to hear that. He felt his smile falter. He'd have to make sure he kept his true emotions off his face tonight, and more importantly, keep himself from voicing them.

Chapter Eight

Maggie couldn't relax, and it had nothing to do with the tense political thriller they'd settled on watching. They'd relegated Jackson to the floor—sort of, his big head was draped over Asher's knee—which gave them the couch to themselves. That could have meant freedom to spread out, except her body seemed to want to be plastered against flannel-and-denim-covered muscles.

She'd given in, tucking herself into his side.

Her heart raced from the closeness. She watched him from the corner of her eye. Light from the action on the screen flashed, casting the angles of his face in colors. They'd discarded their shared popcorn bowl a while ago. He had one hand on the dog's head, and one on her. Arm looped around her back, he drew lazy circles in the hair at her nape. That was partly jacking up her pulse, too. His fingers felt too, *too* good on her neck. She wanted his hands everywhere, spreading that talent to other, more intimate places.

She shut down the thought before her libido took off down that rabbit trail. She took as deep a breath as she could without him noticing. Because as much as he seemed into snuggling, he was remarkably composed. Not sending off any "I could seriously rip your clothes off" signals. Maybe he wasn't ready for that. And she did not need to make a fool of herself by suggesting they try Shirtless Saturday and being rebuffed.

No matter how curious she was to feel his hard muscles under her fingers without his long-sleeved T-shirt in the way.

But with the T-shirt there? That might be okay.

As the on-screen, gun-toting detective wound her way through a Manhattan back alley, Maggie settled her hand below Asher's rib cage. The warmth of the cotton seeped into her skin, promising so much more heat underneath. She splayed her fingers, taking in the ridges of muscle as best she could without full-on groping him.

"Oh, hey!" he exclaimed. She almost pulled her hand back, but then he lifted his chin at the screen, where the detective emerged from the alley and jostled through a crowd in pursuit of her suspect. "I lived not far from that street during my starving-musician days."

"Yeah? I haven't been to New York since I was a teenager."

He shot her a puzzled look. "Doesn't your sister live there?"

"Yeah..." A lie—*I don't like traveling*—sat on the tip of her tongue, but she couldn't voice it. No matter how much the truth hurt. "She's never invited me."

A disapproving whistle ruffled her hair as he kissed the top of her head. "Sorry to hear that."

"Yeah, the Reid penchant for distance runs strong in that one."

And in me.

He was kind enough not to call her on her hypocrisy. "No desire to break the cycle?"

Okay, so maybe he was calling her on it a little bit. He hadn't specified her sister in that challenge. So it was probably directed her way, too.

"Years ago, maybe. But a person gets tired of being turned away after a while. It's easier not to push. Chalk it up to a Stella problem, not a me problem." It hurt less to believe Stella was just afraid to connect after Ryan Rafferty's rejection, that there wasn't something fundamentally unlovable about Maggie. Desperation too readily revealed the truth—Maggie cared more than Stella did.

And Maggie would have been blind not to see that some of the fault didn't lie inside herself. Had it just been her parents who deserted her, it would be one thing. But Stella, too… And then Jeff.

Asher's thumb drew lazy zigzags along the first few vertebrae of her back. "Sounds like your sister's dealing with some rejection issues."

"One could say." She waited for what she thought was an inevitable "and so are you," but it never came.

He just sighed and kissed her forehead. "And it's a shame it's gotten in the way of you seeing New York as an adult. You have some catching up to do."

She let her hand slide a little lower, a subtle exploration of his six-pack. "Where should I start?"

"With food. I could give you a food tour around all the boroughs that would last for months." His voice lowered. "Unless you were referring to starting something with your hand there. In that case, higher, lower, stay where you are—I'm up for whatever."

The sexy growl of his voice hooked her core and pulled her in until there was no possible way she could scramble back. Physically, or situationally—he'd thrown that out there, and it couldn't be erased.

Nor did she want it to be.

"That sounds like way more fun than spending the night talking about my messed-up family."

"I'm happy to show you that I think you're pretty damn awesome." His smile faltered. "But something tells me it would be good for you to open up, Maggie."

Open up.

Yeah, not happening. She'd already said too much. "Something tells *me* it would be better *not* to talk."

His brows knitted. "You just want to finish the movie?"

"Nope." She kissed him. Salt lingered on his lips from the popcorn. He opened his mouth, deepening the kiss, and cola sweetness flooded her tongue. His beard rasped against her chin, and her belly heated.

A cold nose pressed to her cheek.

"Hey!" She nudged the dog's face away. "This doesn't involve you."

Jackson grumbled and sat back down on the floor with a thunk.

Asher chuckled. His fingers explored her back, playing an irregular pattern of whorls and strokes over her sweater and tank top. "And here I accepted your invitation thinking it would be a rare night with no kids interrupting."

She shook her head. "Dogs are the worst. They have no shame. And given the layout of my house—" she motioned a hand toward the archway that connected the living room to the dining area and kitchen "—I can't exactly close the door on him. Though I could put him in the bedroom."

"You could…" Tracing one of her collarbones with a thumb, he studied her, gaze darkening. He dipped in to kiss her again, soft nips that trailed from her lips along her jaw.

She gripped his hard biceps and let her head fall back. "Or we could go to the bedroom."

"Could we now," he said, the words a growl. His lips on her neck, the rasp of his beard on her tender skin, hinted he'd be good with her suggestion.

Being honest about physical need was way easier than having her emotions exposed. She'd pick stripping off clothes to stripping off her protective layers any day. Desire simmered in her veins, dancing along her limbs, pushing her to start with his shirt. Provided that's what he wanted. With his mouth busy kissing her shoulder, she couldn't see his expression to decipher his feelings on the matter.

"If you're up for it," she said casually, running a palm along the firm muscles of his back, walking his T-shirt up with her fingers until the hem bunched in her hand and her fingertips found warm, smooth skin. His muscles twitched under her touch.

He splayed his own hands on her waist and lifted his head. A mix of desire and caution swirled behind his glasses. "I am, but this is a bit odd for me, Maggie. I'm not ending your average dry spell."

She cupped his cheek. She'd been so focused on guarding her own space that she hadn't considered how much of a shift this would be for him. "Is it weird? Being with someone new? Rather... Being with a woman?"

A corner of his lips curved up. "Not in a bad way. Feels pretty damn good. Probably why I'm nervous.

Because I know I'm into you—and I'm good with that—but you don't share those feelings. Not beyond sleeping together, anyway."

Nerves lodged in her throat. That was the problem with this man. Yeah, he turned her on in all the ways. Him shelving books was single-handedly the sexiest thing she'd witnessed in years. And she was desperate to see him with a guitar in his hands. To hear that low voice run up and down some melodic, mellow lyrics as his fingers coaxed out some acoustic magic. But he was so much more than the physical. His ability to make her laugh, his tenderness with his daughter and Jackson, his commitment to life— he could steal her heart if she let him.

Or maybe he'd manage to capture it anyway, even if she didn't want him to.

He watched her, seeming to know she was mulling things over and patiently giving her the time to do that. He stroked a hand along her knee.

"If I don't want anything beyond having my way with you tonight, is that okay?"

His hand paused in its idle path. He rubbed his other palm over his lips. "Normally, I'd say no. I've never been one for casual sex. But maybe that's what I need. A training wheels situation." He winced. "Not that a bike analogy is flattering at all—"

She cut him off by fixing her mouth to his. Swiveling on the couch, keeping her close with a hand at her nape and one at her waist, he landed on his back.

She sprawled on his front, fingers buried in his soft hair. The new angle made her feel everything all at once. The warmth of his body, stretched under hers. Her breasts pressed against his sculpted chest, nipples straining to be freed from the four infernal layers of fabric preventing them from rubbing against his skin. Arousal pooled between her thighs, teased and encouraged by the hard swell of him behind the fly of his pants.

Letting her legs fall to the sides, straddling him, she rocked, centering herself over that tempting ridge.

"Training wheels are okay, then," he murmured in her ear, his breath coming in quick bursts.

They worked for her, too. Maybe he'd be a safe place to test getting a little closer to someone. "They're just fine."

Canine complaints filled her ear as two giant paws landed on the couch next to Asher's head.

She sat up, still straddling Asher's strong hips, and glared at the dog. "You are a menace."

Jackson cocked his head and warbled.

Asher laughed and strong-armed his pet back to the floor. "About that bedroom?"

"Down the hall."

Jackson tried to follow as they made their way from the living room, but Maggie made him stay put with a firm command and a hand signal. With her other hand, she pulled Asher toward her room. Her ranch-style house wasn't overly large. Two bedrooms took up the back half. Hers was decently spacious, and had a set of patio doors that opened to the backyard. She could see having a lazy morning with Asher on her Adirondack chairs.

If he wanted to stay over.

Did he?

She'd leave that question for later. For now, she had more important things to take care of.

Pulling him into her room, she motioned around with her free hand at the king-size bed made with a plush duvet, and the rest of the shabby chic furniture. His head turned slowly as he examined the space with the intent of a university professor conducting a sociological experiment.

"Asher," she complained, tugging him toward the bed. "You're not here to memorize my interior design skills."

"Except I kind of am." He stepped into her space, all heat and solidity and good man scents. "I want to know more about you, Maggie. I'm excited to take you over to that big-ass bed of yours and discover if your skin is as soft as your sweater is, but figuring out what makes you tick is important, too."

Her heart skipped. Half excitement, half panic. She did a quick glance around the room—was there anything he could learn about her here that she didn't want exposed? She'd had guys over before, but none of them had been observant like Asher. They'd been here for one thing, and that's all she'd wanted to give them. But if someone was actually looking… Would he notice how she had pictures of her siblings and grandparents, but not her parents, scattered along her dresser? Was her simple decor the same as a neon *emotionally stunted* sign?

Something close to shame percolated in her stomach, and she dropped her forehead to his chest.

"Stop worrying," he murmured. His finger pressed against her jaw, directing her gaze back to his. "I'm not going to ask anything of you that you don't want to give."

"We can just enjoy tonight?" She stroked his abs, sliding her hands down past his waist and hooking her thumbs under the hem of his T-shirt. The fabric came off too darn easily. Or maybe that was Asher lifting his arms to help, and then tossing the garment in an unceremonious pile over by the rag rug in front of her dresser. His wide chest, exposed and delicious looking right at eye level, teased her senses. She smiled at him and pressed an openmouthed kiss to one of his pecs.

He mumbled his approval before clearing his throat. "Yeah, we can. We *will*."

Spreading his hands wide on her hips, he backed her against the bed and lifted her onto the high mattress, stepping between her legs. One big hand cupped her bottom, pulling her snug to his front.

Even through clothes, the contact seared. She

whimpered and tilted her hips, trying to get closer. "It's too much and not enough all at the same time."

A breath shuddered from his lips and he bent his head to kiss her neck. "I know."

She let her cardigan fall from her shoulders, tilting her head to give him better access to the sensitive skin under her ear. Needing something to do with her hands, she unbuckled his belt and fumbled to unbutton his jeans. But her fingers refused to work properly. She shivered as his facial hair teased her flesh. "Your beard gets an A-plus."

His lips curved against her skin in what felt like amusement. "You're the first to give it a grade."

"I can't be the first to appreciate it, though."

He lifted his head. A visible, naked vulnerability tugged at the corners of his mouth. "I grew it after Alex died. He wasn't much for the mountain man look."

"Oh. I'm…" *Sorry* wasn't the right word. She never wanted him to hold back from talking about Alex. But she hadn't meant her offhand comment to bring up something painful right as he was enjoying himself. "I didn't mean—that is, we don't have to—unless you want to."

"We don't have to what?"

"Talk about your past," she said.

"But it's all tied together, my history and my present," he said, kissing her softly with his hands cradling the sides of her face, fingers just dipping into her hair. Which had to be a mess by now, what with him touching it. Hopefully he liked untamed curls. She had more than her fair share.

She glided her palms down his back, testing the ridges of muscles. Sweet glory, he knew what to do with his mouth. She linked her ankles around his hips and held on for the ride.

After a minute, he drew away and smiled sheepishly. "I want this to be spectacular, but I'm a little out of practice. With anyone for more than a couple of years, because sex wasn't on the table once Alex got sicker. And yeah, pleasure is pleasure and intent matters more than gender, but my last girlfriend was in high school. Which—just tell me what you like, okay?"

"I will." Nerves danced in her belly. "As long as you do the same. I want to be enough for you."

"Of course. And you already are." Fingertips glided along her jaw, leaving a trail of sensation she'd much rather be experiencing between her thighs.

"I—I'm wearing too many clothes," she said.

He lifted a brow. "Back up, Maggie."

She froze. "Uh, you want to slow down? Or go back to talking about—"

"No, I want you to physically back up. I'd toss you onto the mattress myself, but I'm not much for manhandling my partners. Casual is one thing, careless is another."

She scooted against the pillows and studied him,

the hot glint in his eye, the nervous tilt to his mouth. She'd take him at his word that he wanted this, and his agreement that it wouldn't be serious gave her the freedom not to worry about getting attached. But she still needed to be mindful that his first time being intimate with someone after a life-shattering loss was something to cherish. "I think there's room for careful in casual."

He smiled, slow and satisfied. The mattress creaked as he climbed onto the bed and stretched out his long, muscular frame.

"How does vanilla work for you? For now, anyway?" he asked, palming her belly over her shirt.

She rolled into him, hooking a leg over his hips, desperate for more of the exquisite friction that had held so many promises. "Yeah, I can go for that." So long as it involved cozying up on top of her feather bed and pressing her body into his.

His heartbeat thudded against her breasts. Or maybe that was hers?

No, it was both. Almost in rhythm with each other.

The near synchronization jarred her, making her breath catch.

"You okay?" His thumb toyed with her lower lip.

"Yeah, sure." Except she needed to speed this up something fierce. To break away from the soft and emotional, get back to that casual intent they'd set when they were out in the living room and didn't have their hearts echoing each other... Grabbing the hem of her tank top, she stripped it off and pitched it onto the floor. Her pants were next. Then she reached around to remove her bra.

Asher caught her hand before she could reach back and unclasp the garment. "Hey. Let me do that. In a second, though." Slightly slower than she had, he shucked his jeans and socks. Dark hair dusted his legs, and she stroked one of his calves with the sole of her foot.

He traced the top of her bra with a fingertip. A quick circle, and his palm caressed her breast. And his mouth was on her nipple, laving it through the fabric. Need speared her core.

She arched into him. "Ohhh…"

"You like that?"

"Love it."

"Excellent." He kissed his way across to the other side, and she gripped his thick hair, moaning as he pleasured her other breast. "I've been aching to do this." His breath was hot against the wet fabric. "This, too…" His hand played a sweet, torturous trail down her stomach.

"Mmm, I like where you're going," she murmured, tugging on his hair until he brought his lips to hers again. But as his fingers found purchase, slipping inside her panties, she forgot how to kiss. Moaning, though… That happened. Loudly. As did pressing into his hand, a silent plea for more.

If she was going to get out of this without getting dangerously close to attachment, she needed to take charge.

She nudged him onto his back and climbed on top. Oh, yeah. This was so much better without two pairs of jeans muting the heat, the sensation. Nothing emotional. Pure arousal.

Slipping off his glasses, she laid them on the nightstand. His pupils were wide, his chest rising and falling in a quick rhythm. She braced her hands on his pecs and rocked her hips.

His eyes fluttered closed and his lips parted. A low murmur of pleasure rumbled from his chest. Gentle fingers slid her bra straps over her shoulders and he pushed the cups down, coaxing the fabric away from her tender flesh with both hands. Only when he had her squirming from the caresses of his palms did he unfasten her bra, freeing her arms. His thumbs brushed her nipples and she fell against him, mouthing his neck and digging her fingers into his hair.

"One down, one to go," he said teasingly, hooking the edge of her panties and sliding them down an inch. He pushed them to the side and teased her center.

"Mmm, they need to go completely." How the words got out coherently when his fingers were strumming some sort of magic, she didn't know. Limbs heavy and body aching to have all of him, she somehow managed to lift up enough to get the offending cotton off.

"Take mine off, too." A playful smile softened the command.

Dishing him some serious bedroom eyes, she eased the material down. His length sprang against his belly and she licked the tip.

His head fell back on the pillow and he swore.

She explored him with her tongue and lips, circling his base with her fingers as she savored the tastes of salt and man.

"Maggie," he choked out, "I love that, but I can't... Not right now..."

"Too much?"

"Too *good*."

With one last, light press of her mouth to his hot skin, she withdrew and reached into the drawer of her nightstand to get a condom. "I have an IUD," she said, "but we should use this, too."

"Of course."

The second she had him sheathed, his gaze darkened. He flipped her onto her back. Covering her, devouring her mouth.

Overwhelming her with his hands and his chest hair scraping against her nipples and muttering some sort of sweet nonsense, the praise and adoration of a lover...

She gripped his hips, a silent suggestion he get on with things. But he was still kissing her with maddening slowness. Wonderful, yes, but the peak was so close, and she wanted to get there, to fall over the cliff. Just for a moment.

Taking him in hand, she guided him toward her. "Asher, please."

His mouth curved. Oh, he knew what she was begging for. It was obvious he was anticipating it, too. But he was way too content to torture her in the process.

He slid inside her, just an inch or two. Hot and deliciously teasing. She tried to thrust, but he held his hand to her hip to stop her from taking him in further.

"Please, this?" he asked, voice rough and hitching with desire.

"Uh, yeah." She pressed her hips into his grip, needing all of him, needing the fullness. The ache in her core was unbearable. Clutching his broad shoulders, she squeezed her inner muscles.

Groaning, he thrust to the hilt, pausing. His eyes closed and his face slackened with pleasure. "Maggie. Honey, you're… This…" He cursed, low reverence in such a crude word. "Perfection."

"You, too."

His deliberate, unhurried pace obliterated her senses and she lost herself in the movement, in his touch. In savoring the bliss on his beautiful face, the near gratitude.

He kissed her tenderly, tongue matching the rhythm of his strokes. And she kissed him back, trying desperately to feel everything outside without feeling anything inside. Without giving in to the temptation to surrender. How he managed to both soothe and arouse with every rocking, forward drive, she had no idea.

"I need more," she said.

"How?"

"Faster."

"No, love. That's the easy way out. Just let go. Ride it out with me."

"But—"

He snapped his hips harder, cutting off her protest with a wave of pleasure. She was so close, but he clearly needed the sensual pace. And as much as speeding up seemed smarter, safer, how could she resist this? How could she not reach for every scrap of intimacy he was offering? The anxious knot in her chest dissolved and warmth rushed in, building to a breaking point—

One last thrust, and she shattered. A sob escaped her lips and she clung to him, tumbling through the wash of release.

And he followed her, his face buried against her neck, muffling his nonsensical shout.

She splayed her hands on his back. Sweat dampened his skin. Or maybe that was hers, her palms. Heck, her arms and chest and legs.

Lifting his head, he brushed his lips under her ear. "See? Worth going slow."

It was. A sated joy weighted her limbs, and she couldn't hold back a smile. But it was about more than peaking together. It was the safety of his embrace. His solidity, his openness…

All things she could get used to.

Could love.

But she couldn't let herself feel that way.

"Give me a sec," he murmured before withdrawing gently and heading to her en suite bathroom.

Her body chilled. The vulnerability of being alone and naked swept over her, almost as powerful as the orgasm she'd had. She scrambled under the covers. Maybe the layer of feathers and cotton would be enough of a barrier, enough protection.

He strolled back into the room, still naked and as gorgeous as any man she'd ever seen like this. An almost sheepish smile tilted his lips. He motioned to the duvet. "May I?"

She nodded and pulled them back, inviting him into her bed. *And, let's face it, into whatever comes next.*

Because what they'd just shared—that hadn't felt like an end.

This had "beginning" written all over it.

A few hours later Asher woke with Maggie somehow lying sprawled across his chest as well as half the bed. Good thing she had a king mattress.

He smiled to himself. This was comfortable: both the mattress, and the woman he was sharing it with. A warm, irresistible cocoon. Given he wasn't due to pick Ruth up from her sleepover until mid-morning, he was tempted to go shut the lights off—they'd managed to pass out with them on—and stay. Damn, Maggie would look good sleepy and languid, lit up by early sunshine.

She probably wouldn't want that, though. He suspected she hadn't anticipated "sleeping together" would literally mean *sleeping* together. He gave her back a quick stroke, inhaling the berry-sweet scent of her curls, which tumbled over her face and tickled his neck. The alarm clock on her bedside table shone 2:14 in bold, digital blue. He really wanted to stay burrowed under the covers, to better learn the weight of her limbs. But waking up to doubt and awkwardness? Not worth the risk. Better to disappoint her by leaving than by sticking around.

"Maggie?" He shifted out from under her, kissing her forehead as he settled her on one of the pillows and pulled the covers up to her chin. "I should scoot."

"Mmkay," she murmured. One of her brown eyes opened a crack. "You, uh… You could…" She woke up all the way, eyes widening. "Right. Leaving. Not staying. Good call."

He kissed her again before dragging his butt out of bed and putting his clothes back on. She sat up, holding the covers over her naked torso. Her teeth pulled at one side of her lower lip. Concern marked her brows.

"Everything all right?" He put his socks on, studying her.

"Yeah." She squeezed her eyes shut for a second. "Do you want to go out for coffee this week? Or lunch?"

He could hear that the invitation came through gritted teeth, but he got the sense it was her forcing herself to push past her own limitations, not extending it out of a sense of obligation. He mentally scanned his schedule. He was running some of his cultural programming in the afternoons, but that was during his usual hours. Parenting, however, was a total buzzkill when it came to free time. "I have my lunch hours. Other than that, I'm in dad mode every day. Ruth is going to have to put up with doing her homework at the training facility for a few nights so I can get the cabinets done."

And as much as he liked seeing Ruth hero-worship Maggie, he didn't want to introduce Maggie as more than a friend right now. Not until he got a better handle on where this was going and what Maggie wanted. But how to bring that up? There wasn't really a way. Not without freaking Maggie out with words like "commitment" and "step-parent".

Maggie seemed as lost in thought as he was, staring at a point off to his right. After a few seconds, she fixed him with a determined gaze. "I'll come by on Monday at lunch, then."

Excellent. Sure, he'd spend all of tomorrow and Monday morning wondering about her endgame. But future plans were better than her throwing up more walls any day.

Chapter Nine

Maggie had booked herself off for Monday eons ago, needing to go to the dentist and for a physical. The day she'd made the appointments, she'd never have believed she'd spend the morning anxious for her few hours to herself to end so she could see Asher.

Now, all she wanted was for time to pass so she could enjoy his smile and hopefully a kiss or two. Especially since he'd called her just after his shift and started to tell her that library policies would allow her to bring Jackson in as a literacy support animal. Asher had suggested she put Jackson's training vest on him and bring him by when she came for lunch.

He'd told her where to find his spare key, and she now had the dog in tow, having picked him up after her dental cleaning.

Teeth sparkling, health confirmed and toenails painted an appropriate-for-autumn bronze (sue her for squeezing in a pedicure, too, now that there was a chance another human might be looking at her toes) she walked down Main Street toward the library, talking to Emma on her cell.

"You're not getting away with keeping the details from me, Maggie. You spent the night with him," her bestie exclaimed.

Maggie paused. It didn't seem right to spill. The hours of bliss, and the feelings of contentment that followed, were still hard to believe. She needed to keep them close to her heart, give herself time to dwell in them a little more. Not to mention Asher seemed cautious about being a topic of conversation, and she understood why he'd have a heightened awareness.

"What happened after you brought him home?" Emma's glee rang in Maggie's ear.

"He left."

Despite the air temperature diving closer to freezing, Maggie wore flip-flops to preserve her polish job. Their rhythm on the wooden sidewalk sped up in time with her hurrying footsteps. Her pattering heart demanded speed. But walking faster, though calming for her nerves, wasn't going to get rid of Emma's curiosity.

"Yeah, I think you left something out, lady," her friend said.

"We watched a movie." *That we didn't finish.*

"And did the nasty." Emma's tone teased.

"It wasn't nasty." Maggie's chest went all soft and yearning, much like it had yesterday every time she'd felt a wisp of a memory of Asher's hands on her body, his lips caressing and loving.

Emma let out a victorious crow. "Knew it! Guaranteed that man knows what to do between the sheets."

"I'm having lunch with him today, so…"

Silence fell on the other end of the line.

Maggie gripped Jackson's leash as she passed the bakery, where a line was starting to form of locals and tourists looking to dig into one of Nancy Rafferty's double-decker sandwiches for lunch. A few more storefronts, and she'd be at the library. But Emma wasn't going to sign off willingly until Maggie gave her something as equally delicious as the Sweets and Treats chocolate eclair.

"I still have whisker burn," she threw out.

"Where?"

"*Aaaand* would you look at that. I've arrived." The library's automatic door slid open and she entered the foyer. The smells of books and pine-planked walls washed over her. The place was a far cry from when she'd holed up in an old leather armchair in the back corner, burying her nose in a book instead of facing how she felt about her parents unceremoniously dumping her and Lachlan on Gramps and Grams each summer. Or coming with Stella and using one of the computers to research unplanned pregnancies without their grandparents noticing. But all those nooks were long gone—the library had received an airy face-lift years ago. Even so, Maggie imagined it was still a refuge for some.

"Maggie Reid, do not escape into that library!" Emma ordered. "I need details."

"Sign says, 'Quiet,' Emma. Obvs," she whispered.

"Then go back outside!"

"I have a date," she said, still keeping her volume low, hovering in the front foyer by the community announcement board so that she wouldn't disturb anyone.

"I *knooooow*. And I need to know what it is about this guy that's making you go back for more. I mean, I'm all over you going for it. Brava, madam. But he has ropes, not strings attached—"

"Well aware." Maggie took a deep breath to calm the rush of panic that rose at Emma's pronouncement. "When I figure it out, you'll be the first to know, okay?"

Signing off, she put her phone in her purse.

Asher's coworker was behind the circulation desk. Mrs. Brooks was back, tapping away on one of the computers again, this time accompanied by Gertie Rafferty. And the sound of an acoustic guitar providing musical guidance to an off-key group of people singing "Baa, Baa, Black Sheep" filtered around the corner from the children's section.

The guitar switched to a classical Spanish riff, transitioning into a lullaby. That had to be Asher playing. A thrill ran down her limbs. What was it about a man who knew his way around an instrument that was so dang sexy? Trying to look casual, she tightened Jackson's lead and waved at Asher's coworker.

"Hi, Becca," she greeted.

Jackson turned to the librarian and emitted a soft warble, as if he knew he was supposed to be quiet but couldn't help himself.

"I'm going to try a little support training with him," Maggie explained.

"Asher said." The woman grinned. "You can take Jacks over to the baby group if you like. Asher's entertaining them with his guitar."

Aha, it was Asher coaxing out magic with six, measly strings. Sure, it was nursery rhyme magic. But the little trills and flair he added to "You Are My Sunshine" spoke to a rich skill. Good grief, that was enthralling.

She led the dog past the conversation pits to the children's area. Primary colored foam seating, arranged in a horseshoe inside the wall-mounted shelves, created an intimate, cheerful retreat. Asher sat at the crown of a semicircle of parents and their babies. He had their rapt attention.

Especially when his face split in a grin and he launched into lilting, Irish strumming, singing: "I wandered today to the hills, Maggie…to watch the scene below. And something, something, something, Maggie…" He trailed off, finishing in a flourish of strings. "Sorry, I don't know all the words."

Heat washed up her face, a mix of embarrassment and pleasure. That was a whole lot more public than she'd thought him comfortable with. But it was so dang flattering. And adorable. His shy smile warmed her belly.

A dozen curious gazes landed on her, knowing parents, many of whose animals were her patients. And one of whom was her sister-in-law-to-be with her darling niece. Marisol bounced Laura in her lap and studied Maggie with her usual academic intensity.

Her stomach bottomed. Lachlan marrying a psychology expert was usually awesome, but not today. Maggie would have some explaining to do. Nodding at Marisol, she glanced back at Asher.

The interest lighting his eyes almost made her stumble back a step. He had a pair of light green glasses on—so freaking hot. And the casual noodling on the instrument, as if he was playing with-

out even realizing it. Strong, nimble fingers caressed
the neck of the instrument.

Much like they did me.

She bit her lip to keep the memory from showing on her face, but the warmth in her cheeks didn't
dissipate. She smiled sheepishly at Asher before sitting down in the horseshoe and focusing on getting
Jackson to sit. Thankfully, he seemed chill with the
music, patiently waiting while the group sang a goodbye song, and then tolerating the probing hands of
a couple of kids Maggie would guess were around
one year old.

"Gentle," she cautioned. But that was more for
manners than safety—a baby could poke Jackson full
on in the eye, and he'd just sigh and turn his head.

She was looking forward to talking about a new
training schedule over lunch.

*No, you're looking forward to finding a private
place to cozy up with Asher.*

Well, yeah. That, too. She waited for the parents
to clear out. Which was taking forever, considering
Jackson had had three children using him like a jun-
gle gym. Ever the submissive, he flopped on his side
and sighed. After a minute, the parents peeled their
kids off the dog and headed out, but he stayed put.

Marisol made her way over, now wearing Laura
in the same carrier Maggie had borrowed when she
babysat two weeks ago. Panic struck Maggie. One
grilling was enough for the day, and Marisol had "I

have serious questions" written all over her face. But Asher was talking to one of the parents, letting a toddler strum the guitar—oh wow, cutest thing ever—so Maggie couldn't avoid Lachlan's fiancée.

She smiled up at Marisol, struck by the usual pang of envy. Had Maggie wanted to have a baby, she'd have hoped to look as effortless at it as Marisol. She wore the kind of loose bun Maggie was terrible at re-creating, hence her own chin-length haircut. And those comfy leggings and long T-shirt would look like pajamas on Maggie, not runway attire. But Marisol was too darn nice to resent. Lachlan probably spent the majority of his day thanking his lucky stars he'd found a woman whose appearance matched the beauty of her heart.

Maggie'd spent her adult life working to build up her own self esteem after her parents had done their best to strip her of it throughout her childhood. Criticizing her appearance. Breaking promises. Using her affection as a weapon in their animosity-filled marriage. She knew they were wrong, that she had worth. But the patterns were really hard to break sometimes. And she'd never managed to walk through life effortlessly like Marisol did.

Dropping her almost suitcase-size baby bag next to one of the bookshelves, Marisol knelt close to Maggie. "You are not the person I expected to see at Songs and Rhymes."

"I'm not exactly here for the programming,"

Maggie said. What was the point in lying? Heck, what was even the point of salvage mode? It was obvious she'd come to see Asher.

"Oh, I figured that out the minute you got a serenade," Marisol said with a laugh. "That was hot. If your brother had more time for new hobbies, I'd convince him to learn how to play."

"Lachlan's tone-deaf," Maggie said.

"I know." Marisol smiled softly, and Maggie's chest cramped. How did Marisol and Lachlan manage? Being so good with Laura, so good with each other...

They took a risk.

They took a risk, and now were happy. And maybe, given Lachlan had seemed not to internalize their parents' issues like Maggie had, they might even make it work.

And maybe if you actually put some effort into getting over those internalized issues, you could make love work, too.

Ignoring the overly true smackdown from her conscience, Maggie gave her niece's silky hair a quick stroke. "She's going to end up with a head of curls like you and me."

Marisol frowned, ignoring the observation. "What *was* with the serenade?"

"Ask Asher." Heat flared up her neck. "Cancel that, don't. I'll call you later. Just don't tell Lachlan. Or—" she shook her head "—tell him, whatever, I'm not going to ask you to keep secrets from each other. But I don't know what's going on."

"It's okay not to know." Marisol wrapped her arms around Maggie.

Maggie flinched. There weren't that many people in her life who doled out affection, no questions asked.

Marisol immediately drew back. "Sorry. I shouldn't have—"

"No." Maggie returned the other woman's hug, careful not to squish the baby. "It's fine. I... I like it. And I'll call you later."

"Do that."

A pair of casual gray pants materialized next to them, hems crisp over pristine Adidas sneakers. They looked like they might be vintage. Man, Asher's shoe collection was impressive.

"Am I interrupting?" he asked.

"Not at all." Marisol rose and grabbed her bag. "I'm heading out. And I'm holding you to that phone call, Maggie."

She left with a wave and a thank-you to Asher for the class.

Asher settled next to Maggie on the end of the foam horseshoe. He braced his hands on his knees, and his Pearl Jam T-shirt stretched on his shoulders. And now that she knew what he looked like with that shirt off... Actually, it was pretty awesome seeing him fully dressed, too. Naked was lovely, but so was the anticipation of knowing she'd have to wait.

He leaned in close so he wasn't towering over her quite so much. "What about you? Did you enjoy Songs and Rhymes?"

"I'm just glad you didn't sing 'Maggie May.' Rod Stewart does not have a high opinion of that particular Maggie, and I don't need the reminder of how my dad used to quote parts of it—"

Ack, TMI.

Asher's mouth turned down at the corners. "No, not particularly flattering lyrics. Nor do they have anything to do with a father and daughter. Why would he sing that?"

"Oh, who knows with my dad. He thought it was funny." Nor had he realized that she worried that he actually meant it when he sang about wishing he'd never seen her face. Before a lump could form in her throat, she shot to her feet, startling the dog. "Where do you want to go for lunch?"

"Anywhere good, but…" A rare moment when she was taller than him, as he didn't stand. He peered around the library before crooking a finger. "No one's looking." Cupping her cheek, he pulled her in for a kiss. Quick, but it made her knees jelly.

"I can think of a hundred songs that would apply to you," he said.

"What, are you going to make me a playlist?"

"I should." A slow smile spread on his face and he stood, taking Jackson's leash from her. "I will."

"You don't have to."

One of his dark eyebrows arched above his glasses. "You don't want any old-fashioned courting. That answers that."

"I—" Marisol's sappy expression floated back into her mind. As did Asher's steadiness. "Actually, that's exactly what I want. But we have to figure out a couple of things first."

She intended on waiting until they were squirreled away in the corner of the poke restaurant down the street before laying out her thoughts.

Asher had other ideas, though, pinning her with his dilemma the minute they exited the library door into the early October sun, led by the dog. "I feel like I should be guiltier about being willing to find love—or being open to it, I guess would be more accurate. But that was one thing about the months of Alex's health failing—we had a lot of time to grieve together. He downright told me to move on, which helped. When he died… I didn't want that, obviously, but I wanted him to be free of suffering. And he didn't want me to be ruled by grief indefinitely. Plus, it's a cultural thing, so my mom's nudged me in that direction."

"You're too young to be alone for the rest of your life," she replied.

He stopped walking, pulling her toward the window of the bakery and out of the way of the foot traffic. He told Jackson to sit, and the Dane plopped to the ground. "Are you listening to yourself right now?"

"What, you don't think I'm right?"

"No, I do think you're right. And I don't understand why you have completely different rules for yourself than for everyone else. If I shouldn't spend the rest of my life without a romantic partner, why should you?"

"I…" How was she supposed to answer that properly? Honestly?

"Maggie." Dropping Jackson's lead and slipping his hands into her hair, he took her mouth in a kiss that made applause ring in her ears.

Oh, wait, no. Applause was ringing in her ears, because the pair of up-to-no-good senior citizens heading into the bakery were clapping like they were starring in an overzealous internet meme.

Asher tipped an imaginary hat at Mrs. Rafferty and Mrs. Brooks as he picked up the discarded leash. "Ladies."

"Don't stop on our account, dear. News of this will keep the queue at the bakery long all day. Excellent for my daughter's bottom line," Mrs. Rafferty said.

Maggie groaned, and shot the older women a weak smile. "Keep it to a dull roar, okay, Mrs. Rafferty? We have Asher's kid to consider, here."

Asher's abashed smile faded, and he refocused on Maggie as the door swung shut behind the gray-haired duo. "You're right. We need to talk about Ruth."

"I know." She waved a hand at the people inside the bakery pretending not to watch the relationship drama unfolding in front of them. "And this isn't the place for that discussion. You're too citified. You underestimate the number of ears on alert."

He put a hand between her shoulder blades, keeping it there as they started walking again. "You think Brooklyn's any less a fishbowl?"

"New York is huge."

"But the deli a few blocks over from our brownstone wasn't. And don't get me started on the playground by the preschool Ruth used to attend. I see your fishbowl and raise you a rabid shark tank."

She laughed. "Point taken." Hearing about his life back in Brooklyn was lovely, and a good transition into more pressing matters. "I'm starting to see that I'm not being realistic about being alone. And pushing myself out of my comfort zone might be a good thing."

"Okay…" He stared at a point somewhere down the block for a good thirty seconds, far beyond the coffee shop and ski apparel stores they were passing. He came to a halt in front of the poke restaurant and told Jackson to stay, scratching him between the ears. They were planning to eat outside on the heated patio so they could have the dog next to them, tied to the railing.

"Look," he continued. "I know you're not sure about a relationship. And when it comes to my feelings, I'm a grown man. I can take it. But—" He blew out a breath. "I can't believe I have to say this, given it's crazy early. Then again, I've never dated as a father." His serious brown gaze delved deep, past her inhibitions and fears. "If we test the waters for a while, and decide to make some sort of commitment to each other, is there room in your life for Ruth? I know you don't want kids. The fact I have one—is that a nonstarter?"

"Well…" Was it? She'd never wanted a baby. But a ten-year-old who was already articulate and interesting and her own person… That was entirely different. "I don't think so. But it's also something I need to think on. Is that okay?"

He nodded. "Of course."

"I could ask you the same question, you know. As someone who has a child, would you theoretically be okay not having more?"

Another nod, this time making a strand of near-black hair fall across his glasses. He pushed it back. "I don't need to think on that—I've only ever seen myself having one child."

"Okay, then." Her chest felt oddly light. "Good talk. I can honestly say this was a new one for me.

Can we, uh, not be serious for the rest of our lunch? I feel we've hit our quota for, like, a month."

"You got it. And, Maggie? Take your time. We don't need to be in a hurry. I'm not going anywhere."

And if she could convince herself that was true, it might make moving forward actually possible. But digging out from under a lifetime of doubt and pain wasn't going to be possible in a day. What if she pushed herself and he wasn't able to be there in the end because Ruth wasn't ready to see him with someone who wasn't Alex? What if *he* started dating someone Maggie and then realized she couldn't live up to his late husband?

Cross out one doubt at a time, Maggie. Just have lunch with the guy.

She inhaled, trying to settle her stomach. Finally, some good advice from the recesses of her brain. Lunch wasn't everything, and she definitely couldn't make any guarantees yet, but it seemed like a good place to start.

Asher spent most of the next week and a half stealing as many private moments with Maggie as he could. He had Ruth with him whenever he worked on the barn, which meant platonic encounters, but nothing like what he and Maggie had shared the one shift he'd managed to be alone. She'd come to the library to have lunch with him a couple of times, but that didn't allow anything close to their one night of pleasure. And he was aching to make love to her again. But figuring out when to make that happen was tricky, given they weren't being open with anyone about seeing each other, and he couldn't leave Ruth to fend for herself while he snuck off with his girlfriend.

Girlfriend. Was Maggie his girlfriend? Who knew?

At least cabinet building gave him a ton of time to ponder it. And to realize that he sure as hell wanted to call her that. The conversation they'd had about parenting had given him hope. Dropping that on her had been necessary—and more than a bit awkward— but she hadn't turned on a heel and walked away. For someone seemingly petrified of being vulnerable, she seemed to understand his unique position.

He made sure to get together with his brother for a mid-week run. He needed someone to talk to, and getting advice from his friends in Brooklyn felt awkward. They'd only ever known him with Alex, and he didn't know how they'd react to him finding someone new, who happened to be a woman. Running on an isolated trail was an easy place to be honest, and Caleb was an excellent listener.

"Am I being unrealistic, here?" Asher asked, his running shoes beating an even rhythm on the dirt trail behind Caleb's house. "Trying to date so soon after moving?"

Caleb snorted. "I'd be a hypocrite if I told you not to."

"True." Caleb had found love with Garnet only a few months after arriving in Sutter Creek.

"Also," his brother continued, "I'm in Mom's camp. There are ways to learn to live after loss or big changes. And love is often the best choice."

"I've always tried to believe that."

"You have more things to think about than many people do—being widowed and having a daughter, of course, but beyond that? You're looking at a relationship with a woman, for one. That's not a small change. And she's white, and isn't Jewish. Complications. Worth it—I'm happy as anything with Garnet. But it still requires thought."

"I know, and I'm not discounting all that. But I don't think we're even there yet. I'm afraid I'll put myself out there and she'll decide she's not ready to commit."

"An exceedingly intelligent man once told me that love was worth the risk of loss."

Asher arched a brow at his brother and elbowed him, throwing Caleb off his stride. He slowed, waiting for Caleb to right himself. "I still do believe that. It's a matter of convincing Maggie of the same."

Caleb slowed to a walk and put a hand on Asher's shoulder. "What draws you to her?"

"Her passion for her job, her family, the community. The way she interacts with Ruth. The fact

I feel comfortable talking to her about pretty much anything."

"Then talk to her about this when the time is right."

Good advice, but finding that right time wasn't easy given their busy schedules.

Halloween fell on a Friday, and he spent the evening following Ruth and her friends around their neighborhood. His daughter was dressed up in Hogwarts robes, complete with a blue-and-silver knitted scarf. Harper's and Fallon's scarves were red and gold. And Ruth had fashioned a black cape and black-and-yellow scarf for Jackson. She'd convinced Asher to put in his contacts and wear a round pair of prop glasses, and had drawn a lightning scar on his forehead. They'd done a full two-hour circuit and had dropped Ruth's friends at their houses, pillowcases full of candy, when Ruth tugged on the sleeve of the robes he'd worn for library dress-up events back in Brooklyn.

"Can we go to Maggie's house, Dad? I want to show off Jackson's costume."

He glanced down at his Hogwarts attire. Some people might roll their eyes at him getting dressed up to trick-or-treat with his kid, but Maggie wasn't one of them. "You're not tired, peanut?"

Ruth let out a puff of exasperation. "I'm *ten*. I can stay up late on Halloween now."

He held up his hands in surrender. He wasn't

about to ruin her fun. Besides, it would give him a chance to at least see Maggie, even if he wouldn't get the chance to kiss her with Ruth around. "Maggie's house, it is."

They drove over, Jackson taking up the two-thirds of the back seat not occupied by Ruth. Maggie's porch light was still on when they pulled into her driveway. The dog went on alert, jamming himself between the two front seats and wagging his whole body.

"Easy, buddy. You'll get to see your lady friend."

Then again, his figurative tail was wagging just as hard as Jackson's.

Ruth ran up and knocked on the door.

Maggie answered, one arm filled with a bowl of candy, the other with a smaller bowl of dog treats. Scanning Asher from his glasses to the hem of his robes, she grinned.

"Trick or treat!" Ruth exclaimed.

"One for you—" juggling the bowls, Maggie dropped a handful of mini Aeros in Ruth's pillowcase before making Jackson sit for a cookie "—and one for you."

"And for me?" Asher asked, unable to keep a hint of suggestion out of his voice.

"Candy bar or dog cookie?" Her mouth twitched. "You've earned a treat."

He plucked a wrapped chocolate out of the bowl, opened it and popped it in his mouth. "Have I?"

The porch light was just bright enough to betray her pink cheeks. "You're an excellent wizard. The three of you have made my night. Your costumes are perfect."

"I have a wand, too." Ruth brandished the decorative stick and made a flourish with her hand. "Stupefy!"

Maggie pretended to freeze, before placing the bowls on the narrow table in her entryway. She knelt to snuggle the dog. Her gaze lifted to Asher, promise flecking gold in her brown irises.

"Lots of trick-or-treaters?" he asked, wishing he didn't have to make idle conversation. Wishing he could lean in and greet her with a kiss.

"About fifty kids," she said, running her tongue along her lower lip.

He groaned silently. Damn. One night to end his dry spell had started a flood—he wanted this woman in his bed every night. And it had been two weeks since they'd slept together. He was going to need to get Caleb and Garnet to take Ruth for a night soon so that he could have a quiet date in with the woman currently devouring him with her gaze.

Ruth bounced on her toes. "Maggie, can I use your bathroom?"

"Second door on the left," Maggie said, waving an arm toward the hall.

The second the latch clicked, she was in his arms, her lips on his and her fingers in his hair.

One brush of her body against his front and he hardened.

"I need to touch you more, Asher," she complained, voice low and sultry. "A few minutes here and there in Lachlan's office just isn't cutting it."

He groaned his agreement. "I think it's time for me to talk to Ruth. She was comfortable enough to want to share her Halloween costume with you. That's a good sign. If I frame it gently, I think she'll be open to the idea of me taking you on a date now and then. That'll give us the occasional evening to ourselves." He stole another kiss, savoring the sweetness lingering on her lips. "You pilfered candy from the bowl."

"Of course I did." She took a step back, linking fingers with him and staring at their joined hands. "Yeah, I think I'm ready to be more open with Ruth, so long as you can figure out an age-appropriate way to express that we're very much just dating. I don't want her to get the impression that I'm trying to horn in on her relationship with you. Or take Alex's place. Or that what we have is something serious."

A warning bell clanged in the little protective center at the back of his head. "But if we decide to stop seeing each other, I'm concerned how Ruth will handle you walking out of her life."

Maggie's eyes widened, stricken. "I wouldn't do that to her. I'd find a way to still be in her life. I know how important it is not to desert a child. Why do you think I've been so nervous about the idea of commitment?"

"I honestly assumed it was more about self-protection," he said, squeezing her hand.

"Well, it's that, too," she murmured. "But it's also about Ruth. And the dog... I have plans for him. I want to train him so he can do that literacy work I mentioned."

As if he understood the word *dog*, Jackson bumped against their linked hands. Asher gave the big guy an ear scrub. Asher loved the idea of having a literacy dog at the library—he'd been working on making the idea a reality ever since Maggie had brought it up. Jackson had responded well to the couple of hours Maggie had fit in with him. "Well, I'll broach the subject with her."

"What subject?" a small voice said from behind him.

Asher spun toward his daughter, who had reappeared in the entryway. She was straightening her robes and scarf, brows furrowed.

His gut shimmied. "Let's head out, Ruth."

By the time he got his daughter home and had her de-Pottered and sitting on the couch with Jackson's head draped across her knee, the shimmy had escalated into a full roll. Ruth had a mouthful of one of the specialty Kit Kat bars his dad had picked up in Japan on his last trip to visit his cousins. He'd mailed two so that Asher and Ruth could enjoy their usual

Matsuda Halloween tradition, but Asher's stomach was too unsettled for candy.

"You know how Papa talked to you about me eventually wanting to have a partner again?"

She worried one of the dog's ears with her thumbs. "Yeah…"

"Well, I'm interested in having someone in my life. Which is obviously something that affects you."

"Are you talking about Maggie?" she asked, face screwed up in thought.

"I am. I'd like to get to know her better, as more than friends."

"You mean being her boyfriend?"

"That's the idea."

She sucked her upper lip between her teeth. "Are you going to marry her?"

"I don't know, honey. We're not thinking about that right now. We'd need to go on a lot of dates, first. We'd need to spend time together, all three of us, too. You get a say in this. I'm not going to bring someone you're not comfortable with into your life. And you and I both need to be ready for things not to be a guarantee. Sometimes when adults date, they decide it's not working."

"I'm not stupid," she scoffed. "I know that. I have, like, four friends whose parents are divorced."

He nodded. "I just wanted to tell you so you weren't surprised."

"I saw you hugging her when we picked Jackson up. I knew you liked her."

Good thing he'd talked to Ruth today, then. He wouldn't have wanted her to be sitting and wondering, too nervous to ask. He also had to assume she had questions about him being with someone who wasn't a man, too. He and Alex had talked about sexuality and gender identity many a time over the years, but it wouldn't hurt to check. "You've never seen me in a relationship with a woman, so if you need to get used to that, it's okay."

"I know you like boys and girls, Dad. People can like whoever they like."

He smiled. "Glad you think so."

"But—" Her face crumped.

"What, honey?"

She tucked herself against him, burying her face in his chest. "You won't love Papa anymore."

The words were muffled, but the sentiment got across in every syllable. And was a damn bullet to the heart.

He snuggled her close. "I'll always love him. That won't go away. It's not about letting go of him. It's about making space for new people."

And so long as Maggie opened up to him more, he could see having space for her in his life for a long, long time.

Chapter Ten

Late Tuesday afternoon, Asher checked his pockets for his keys, about to leave their town house to drive Ruth into Bozeman for Hebrew school at their synagogue.

"Why are we leaving Jackson at home?" his daughter asked, tone suspicious.

"Because Maggie's coming with us. Remember how I wanted the three of us to spend time together? And she and I are going to go to the hardware store while we're waiting for you." And planned on going out for dinner. Even though he and Ruth had talked about him dating, he didn't want to force the issue. If she asked, he'd be honest. But he wasn't going to wave his dates with Maggie in his daughter's face. Tough, given all he wanted was to touch and kiss and tease Maggie in that obviously intimate, we're-a-couple way that an overly analytical ten-year-old would cotton onto in a second.

Frowning, Ruth checked her backpack. Asher knew the routine. Notebook, stuffed dragon, quidditch pencil case. And the ribbon-tied packet of letters Alex had written to Ruth. The scan must have passed muster, because she zipped up the bag and slung it over her shoulders.

"Why does Maggie coming mean Jackson can't?" she asked. "He loves her."

"But he won't love getting left in the car."

His daughter said a dramatic and elongated good-bye to the dog, and sulked in the back seat on the short drive to Maggie's.

Maggie was waiting on the porch, and as she slid into the front seat, he leaned forward to give her a kiss. Oh, crap. So much for being on guard. He tried to cover the instinctual action by leaning into the back seat and grabbing a tissue out of the box on the floor of the car. He caught Ruth's quizzical gaze out of the corner of his eye. Schooling his expression, he straightened and pretended to blow his nose. Hopefully that hid the freaking joy jumping in his chest at the mere sight of Maggie with her curls held back with pins and face framed by the swoopy scarf wrapped around her neck.

Blowing your nose before the second date even starts. Way to be hot, Matsuda.

But the unattractive move was better than kissing Maggie in front of his daughter, so he'd have to eat the embarrassment.

Maggie turned to greet Ruth, and her gaze homed in on Ruth's long face. "Why so sad, kiddo?"

"Dad left the dog at home."

"I'm glad to hear you like spending time with him," Maggie said carefully. "But it's okay for him to be alone sometimes. He likes his crate."

"He'd better—it's taking up a third of our living room," Asher mock complained.

"You didn't adopt a Chihuahua, that's for sure." Maggie laughed. "So, tell me about how our techniques are going, Ruth."

Ruth brightened as she launched into a minute-by-minute rundown of the practice she'd put in with Jackson since her class with Maggie. He drove, shaking his head a little. It felt like they were running on alternate timelines. One where he had to keep Ruth's needs in mind, slowly easing into a relationship with Maggie. And his, where it had been over two weeks since he'd gotten to spend the night in Maggie's bed and he was eager to ease back between those sheets with her.

Once Ruth exhausted her Jackson stories, she fell back into near silence, despite Maggie's attempts to draw her into conversation. Asher glanced at her in the rearview mirror. His daughter's cheeks were flushed, and she was hugging her rib cage. Was she still bothered by the dog being left at home? Or had she picked up on him almost kissing Maggie? They were almost at the synagogue, and with Maggie in the car, it wasn't possible to have another State of the Family discussion.

"You okay, peanut?"

"My tummy hurts a little."

Damn. He hated to think she was having a resurgence of the physical grief symptoms that had plagued her for the first year after Alex's death. She'd been doing so well, especially with the addition of Jackson to the family and with the promise of ski lessons. Had he disrupted that progress by putting him dating on the table? He shared a quick glance with Maggie. Her mouth twisted in sympathy.

"You going to be okay for Hebrew school?" he asked.

Ruth looked out the window and nodded, her hair falling in a sheet across her cheek.

"Have I told you about the puppy I'm going to be training next, Ruth?" Maggie asked.

His daughter shook her head.

"I was supposed to get her today, but I have to wait for two more weeks. She's sixteen weeks old. A chocolate Lab. I'm going to assess her to make sure she has the right temperament—personality and attitude—to support someone with autism. You said you had a friend in New York with an autism support dog, right?"

"Yeah." The tiny voice was barely audible from the back seat.

"They're very useful. All support animals are. You know who's the funniest working animal in Sutter Creek?"

"No." Another whisper.

Asher's chest clenched, and he tried to watch his daughter and the road at the same time.

"Well, Beverley's not technically a service animal—pigs don't qualify—but he definitely thinks he's a lapdog. All 90 pounds of him. And he helps his owner with her anxiety, so they're a good match. But seeing a potbellied pig on a pink harness and leash never fails to make the tourists do a double take."

Asher smiled, and damn, did he appreciate Maggie's efforts, but Ruth wasn't going to thaw. She gave a half-hearted "That's cool," and dug in her backpack, taking out her dragon and the letters. She spent the rest of the drive rubbing a dragon's wing between a thumb and forefinger and clutching the packet in her other hand.

Asher and Maggie made small talk about the last few things he had to finish for the interior of the training barn, including the cabinet handles that they needed to exchange before dinner.

He pulled into the parking lot and into a visitor's

spot. "We'll just be a minute," he said to Maggie, who nodded in understanding.

"Ruthie," he said, after they were both out of the car and walking toward the front door. He put his arm around her narrow but sturdy shoulders. "What's on your mind?"

"Papa. And my stomach ache."

He tucked her hair behind her ears. "Want to talk about it?"

"I have class."

"You feeling good matters more," he assured her. "If you're not okay, we can head home."

She shook her head, canceling out his efforts to keep her hair tidy. "I'm fine. And you don't have to walk me. I know the way."

He gave her a quick kiss on the cheek, and she scurried off, head ducked and thumbs looped in her backpack straps.

His deep breath failed to ease his concern, and he walked out to the car, legs heavy. He slid into the driver's seat and gripped the wheel.

"Hey." Maggie settled a hand over one of his. "I thought you said Ruth seemed okay with us dating."

He released the wheel with one hand so that he could link fingers with Maggie. "She did. Something set her off about leaving the dog at home, though."

"She hasn't confided in you?"

"Not yet. She often needs a day or two to mull over whatever's bothering her."

odded. "She knows she can trust you, Asher. Tha◼◼h is obvious. No way would I have let my dad put his arm around me when I was mad at him."

"Well, that's something. You think I should dial down the paranoia?"

"You're having to compensate for being her only living parent. Having extra worry is probably normal. I just wouldn't panic about her having a quiet moment," she said.

"Okay." Maybe the wave of guilt that he still wanted time alone with Maggie was overkill, too, then. Or at least he'd tell himself that so that he could enjoy the next couple of hours. "Hardware store first?"

"Yeah, and after, I have somewhere to show you."

"No dinner? I wanted to take you out to a nice restaurant. Somewhere without a platoon of well-meaning senior citizens breathing down our necks."

"I don't need anything fancy. I just like spending time with you. Let's hit up a drive-through and then I'll take you for a tour."

Which is how he ended up full to the brim with a double cheeseburger and fries, parked under a private overhang of trees by the river a few minutes out of town. Lap full of woman. He'd left the keys in the ignition and the battery on, some folk rock setting the mood.

"You're sure this is private enough?"

"A friend of mine owns this property. No one'll come down here."

"Maggie Reid," he murmured, kissing a line from her throat to her ear. "Are you taking advantage of me?"

"You seem like you need to loosen up, Asher. And while I don't think you're wrong to try to suss out what's on Ruth's mind, she's busy at the moment."

He cupped one of her breasts and flicked her hardening nipple with his thumb. She whimpered.

"So we should get busy, too?" he asked.

"I've had worse ideas." She circled her hips over his half-hard penis, and pleasure rushed downward. Man, he could get used to having her straddle him in the front seat of his car. He would dearly love to throw himself off an emotional cliff with this woman, but until she was more comfortable, that would be like jumping without a parachute—

"Asher?" Stilling her movements, she blinked and palmed his chest. "Are you not into this?"

"Uh, you can't tell?"

"An erection isn't consent. And you seem distracted." Her teeth tugged at her lower lip,

"Sorry, love. I'm fully yours. So long as some deputy isn't about to come arrest us for public indecency."

"Promise, we're alone."

Kissing her, delving under her shirt and bra with his hands, he did his best to prove he was willing to take advantage of their privacy. Her body was strong, from working with animals, no doubt, but she had a hell of a lot of soft parts, too. And his hands were still getting used to that, to the feminine. He loved touching her. Exploring her curves, coaxing out moans. And discovering how wet she was when he slipped his fingers under her skirt and shifted her panties to the side.

He groaned his appreciation and teased a languid pattern on her slick flesh. "You feel so good, Maggie."

She squirmed against his hand, gripping his shoulders hard enough for her short nails to sting through his shirt. "Not…quite…good enough…"

"Can't have that." Rubbing her nub with his thumb, he thrust two fingers inside her wetness and pressed her inner wall. He settled his mouth over hers, a deep kiss mimicking the rhythm of his hand.

Her mouth fell away as she cried out, her sex pulsing around his fingers. Heat pooled in his groin, the satisfaction of having helped her find her release fueling the desire to find his own. He withdrew his hand and gave her back a stroke.

Chest heaving, she pressed her forehead against his shoulder. "Now *that* was enough," she mumbled.

"Sounded like—"

His ringing phone, connected to his hands-free system, interrupted. He glanced at the display. "Ah, crap, it's the synagogue."

Maggie stilled in his lap, and he answered.

"Asher? It's Jill Kaufman." Ruth's teacher's voice rang with concern. "How far away are you? Ruth got sick to her stomach during the history lesson."

His own nausea reared at the teacher's news— guilt induced, of course. Killed his sexual desire, too. Damn it. He never should have sent Ruth tonight. Had he let the time with Maggie cloud his judgment?

After assuring Ms. Kaufman that he'd be there in ten minutes, he hung up, and helped Maggie over the console and back into the passenger seat. They both straightened out their clothes. He peeled out of the riverside site, driving as fast as he could get away with.

"Sorry, Maggie," he said, rubbing his chest. Where was his container of antacids when he needed it?

"Don't apologize. I just hope she's okay. Want me to drive home so you can sit with her in the back seat?"

"Maybe."

Ruth's spiking temperature answered that question for him. He let Maggie take over the wheel so he could be closer to his now-feverish daughter. She rested her head in his lap on the trip back to Sutter Creek, dragon tucked under her chin.

"You must have a stomach bug, Ruthie. Sorry I didn't notice," he said. Though part of him was almost happy it was a virus—maybe her gastrointestinal troubles were unrelated to her mental health.

Even so, between missing her illness and having to cut his date with Maggie short, he was letting down the people he cared about on all sides tonight.

"Sorry I threw up. The garbage can was too far away, and I made a mess on the floor." Tears sparkled in her eyes. "Some of the other kids laughed. The rest ran to the other side of the room."

"That's rotten, honey. They'll forget by next week, though. Everyone throws up in public at some point."

He wasn't paying much attention to where they were going, so when Maggie pulled into his driveway, he startled. "I'll drop you off, Maggie. It's freezing out."

She shook her head and got out of the car, snatching her purse from the floorboard as she exited. "I have gloves and a hat—I'll walk home. You take care of your sick one."

He lifted a corner of his lips and slid out himself, taking Ruth's backpack with him. His daughter wobbled a bit when she stood, and he went to her, lifting her into a spider monkey hug like he'd done when she was a preschooler.

Maggie unlocked their front door and rubbed Ruth's back. "Call me later?"

"Yeah." He loved the idea of ending the day with a phone call. He just wasn't sure Ruth was actually ready for Maggie being in his life.

Hours passed before Asher got the chance to call Maggie like she'd asked. Having been unable to convince Ruth to have a piece of dry toast, he'd settled for getting her to take in as much electrolyte drink as he could. Instead of going to an after-hours clinic, his brother had come by to check on Ruth. He and Caleb ended up chatting and playing fetch with the dog in the backyard for an hour after Ruth fell asleep.

By the time his brother left and he showered off the sickbed grime, it was already past ten. Instead of risking waking Maggie up, he sent her a text, asking if she was awake.

He was going to need to apologize—with Ruth ailing, he'd be housebound tomorrow night, which would put him behind on the renovation project. Garnet was saving his ass when it came to finding child care—she'd volunteered to spend her day off with Ruth so that he could work his usual Wednesday shift at the library—but he couldn't justify working through the evening as well, or taking Ruth along with him while she felt so crummy. Which would mean being short for the fees that were going to be due for the ski club in a couple of weeks. To borrow one of Maggie's phrases, fudge crackers.

She replied a minute or so later.

I'm in bed, but awake.

He smiled. The possibility of ending off the night with conversation rather than vomit and money worries was welcome. As was the mental picture of

Maggie in bed. A teeny pair of sleep shorts would showcase her toned legs in all the right ways.

He dialed her number.

Maggie answered on the first ring and settled against her pillow, sure to add extra innuendo to her tone. "What are you wearing?"

Laughing, he replied, "Afraid I sleep fully clothed. T-shirt and boxers."

Mmm. Hot. "You say that as if you in a T-shirt and boxers is a bad thing."

"Flattery will get you everywhere, Maggie Reid."

"Too bad it can't get us in the same bed." She sighed. She felt badly that she hadn't gotten the chance to make him feel as good as he had for her, before they got interrupted. "How's Ruth doing?"

He gave her a rundown of his evening, then paused awkwardly.

"Everything okay?" she asked. Ruth had been irritable at times on the car ride to Bozeman, and she wanted to be sure the mood had been illness-related, not caused by Maggie's company.

Asher cleared his throat. "I'm not going to be able to come in tomorrow to finish up Lachlan's office. It's going to push it forward a few days, because Thursday is parent-teacher night at Ruth's school and then Friday's family night, and Saturday there's a Shabbat service…"

Maggie sucked in a breath. "It's okay."

"Are you sure?" he asked. "Doesn't sound like

it's entirely fine. I'll give your brother a call tomorrow to explain."

She rushed to correct his misinterpretation of her tone. "The schedule change is honestly not a problem. I'll tell him. He has classes next week, but as long as he gets the multipurpose area set up for then, I'm sure he'll be okay if his office is in shambles."

"I don't like not being able to follow through."

She paused. She had to ask him about Ruth, otherwise she'd never get to sleep. "Speaking of follow through, I wanted to make sure you still think this is a good idea. Ruth was less than happy to see me today."

"Right, uh, I don't think there's anything to worry about, but we can talk more if you want. Do you want to video chat me instead?"

"What, so you can destroy my sense of reason with a smile and a wink? I seem to be pretty weak when it comes to your face, Asher. Especially when you're wearing your glasses." Which was most of the time, given he rarely wore contacts.

"I'll keep the winking to a minimum."

"And smiling?"

"No guarantees. It seems to be my natural state when you're around."

Her heart pattered.

They connected via the app thirty seconds later, and his appreciative half grin filled her phone screen.

Pushing up his glasses with a finger, he winked at her "Hey."

"Told you not to do that."

"Not happening, Maggie. I might be tired, and it might take me days to get the scent of puke out of my nostrils, but you make me happy."

"That's…" She glanced away from her phone. Ugh, it was harder to guard her feelings over a video connection.

He didn't fill the silence, though, and she appreciated the time to gather her thoughts.

"I didn't like Ruth being grumpy with me today," she confessed.

"I know," he said. "But she was coming down with the flu. I'm pretty sure that her mood was from her feeling sick, not her opinion on our relationship."

"If you say so. I have no frame of reference. I mean—" she stared into his understanding gaze "—how am I supposed to know how to raise a child? I had the worst example."

He nodded slowly. "Is that why you don't want to have a baby of your own?"

"No," she said. "I just—I'm not a baby person. That was never going to be for me. I find it easier to connect with older children. Whether or not I would be any good in a parent role, though? I'm going to need some time."

He rubbed his cheek, smoothing out his beard.

Dang, this conversation would be so much easier

if she was lying next to him, running her own fingers along his facial hair.

"That's fine," he said. "I explained to her there were no guarantees."

Her chest cramped at his words. "It doesn't seem like enough. Are you sure it's okay?"

"I'm sure that I like seeing you. And that I want to keep doing that, even if it means having to stop myself from kissing you in the car like I had to earlier tonight. I lose my head a little when I'm around you, Maggie."

"You do the same to me." She couldn't tell him everything she was feeling. But that little admission seemed a fair compromise. And the smile it earned her kept her happy for days.

By Saturday morning, Ruth was on the mend.

Asher, however, was hanging over the toilet, wishing he'd never heard of such things as breakfast and coffee.

"Dad?" His daughter hovered outside the bathroom door. "Guess we're not going to temple this morning?"

"Sorry, peanut." He dragged himself to the sink and rinsed out his mouth. "That's going to be a no. Movie marathon?"

He spent the day in a blur of Netflix and flu symptoms. Ruth got a crash course in paying for delivery pizza, lest Asher pass the bug on to the unsuspecting delivery person, and they both went to bed early, Ruth still being tired from three days of the flu. Asher was up most of the night, glad he had an en suite so he didn't disturb his daughter across the hall. He woke up Sunday morning, a sweaty, shaky mess.

No way was he going to be able to go into the clinic and knock off the rest of the finishing work in Lachlan's office. His stomach clenched, from guilt and disappointment instead of nausea.

He'd have preferred nausea. Letting down Maggie and her brother made him feel like an absolute heel.

After a shower, he shuffled to the living room and downright oozed onto the couch across from Ruth, who was lying curled on the floor with Jackson, watching a Disney cartoon. An empty bowl sat on the coffee table beside her with the dregs of milk and Alpha-Bits—her weekend treat—in the bottom.

"You look like you're going to puke again." She studied him, dark eyes full of concern. "I don't think we should go to Maggie's today."

"I don't either," he croaked. He'd have to call and cancel, and then figure out where he could make up the time. Damn it. Lachlan was supposed to be holding a class there tomorrow.

Dialing Maggie's number, he sandwiched his cell between the cushion and his ear so that he didn't have to hold his gelatin-muscled arm up for any length of time.

"Morning, sunshine," she greeted, sounding disgustingly chipper. "When are you coming to work? I might head to church this morning. My friend Emma is playing the piano for her mom, who's singing. I like to go for moral support. You'll probably be started on the last cabinet doors by that point."

He tried to reply with words, but a low groan came out instead. "Maggie, I…"

"What's wrong?"

"Nothing big, I just—"

"Cut the crap." She spoke with the firmness of a medical professional well used to getting emergency phone calls from people dealing with illness. Animal sickness, mind you, but ailing creatures just the same. "You're sick."

"As a dog. Better to be a dog, really. You could medicate me."

"You don't want to call Caleb?" she suggested.

"Just a virus. Need to sleep it off." He glanced at his daughter. Aside from crapping out on Lachlan and Maggie, he was cheating Ruth out of her weekend, too. And the dog would need to be walked. He groaned again. Where was his get-out-of-adulting-free card?

"I'm coming over," Maggie announced.

"You don't have to."

"You need me to," she insisted.

She was right. He so did. "Thanks, love," he murmured before hanging up.

His eyes fluttered closed, and God, just a little sleep would do wonders… Like, maybe a week or so.

"Daddy?" Ruth whispered.

"Mmm-hmm?"

"You called Maggie 'love.'"

Oh, hell. He didn't have the energy to sit up, let alone navigate another complex conversation about grief and love and moving forward. He cracked one eye open. "I did, Ruthie." Not exactly a lie. Why he'd started to use the endearment when he'd never used it before in his life, he didn't know. The other options—*babe, sweetheart, beautiful*—didn't seem quite right for Maggie, though. "It's just a nickname."

Also not a lie. Had he been thinking, he would have waited to use the word in front of Ruth.

"Do you…" Her face screwed up on one side, and she curled up tighter against the dog, who lifted his head to lick her cheek. "Do you love Maggie?"

His heart launched into his throat. "Not yet, honey. Are you okay with her helping us today?"

"*I* can help you. I can make toast and tea. Or soup."

"I know. And we're a good team. But you need a functioning grown-up around."

Her face clouded with anger. "If we hadn't moved, then Grandma could help."

Oh, he had no doubt of that. His mom had bent over backward trying to help Asher and Ruth after Alex's death. But she'd supported his decision to take a new job, as well as his hope that somewhere new would be a good foundation for a new start.

Had he made the right choice? Seeing the uncertainty and mistrust on Ruth's face, unable to even sit up because his muscles felt like they were made up of processed meat—how was he supposed to stay optimistic about his decisions?

He wasn't going to begrudge Ruth her moment of wishing for her grandmother. Hell, a bowl of his mom's miso matzo ball soup sounded exactly right.

His stomach churned at the thought.

Okay, correct that. It would be the perfect remedy in another day or so when he was able to smell food without gagging.

"You want to give Grandma a call, honey?"

She nodded.

After unlocking his cell with a weak press of his pointer finger to the sensor, he handed her the device. "Help yourself."

Ruth took the phone, and a short time later was chattering happily to her grandmother. Dramatically recounting their bout with illness, more accurately. Great, his mother was going to worry that he'd was on death's door by the way Ruth was describing his symptoms.

"I'm fine, Mom," he called feebly.

"He's *gray*, Grandma." Ruth wandered out of the living room and in the direction of the kitchen, Jackson on her heels.

"You're way too cheerful about my suffering, Ruth."

She paused in the kitchen doorway and turned to him. "You'll be okay in a couple of days, Dad. I'm fine now."

He should be counting his blessings, really, that she was being so relaxed about him being sick. The last time Ruth had seen a parent stricken with nausea, it had been Alex during chemotherapy treatment.

"I don't know where Uncle Caleb is." Ruth cocked her head, clearly listening to something his mom was saying. "No, Dad's *girlfriend* is coming over."

Oh, hell. He held out his hand. "Ruth, let me talk to Grandma."

"He wants to talk to you," Ruth relayed. A long silence followed. "Okay, bye!"

He lifted a brow at his daughter. No way had Ruth's use of *girlfriend* not aroused his mom's curiosity. She must have decided to take pity on his flu-ridden self. "She didn't want to say hello to me?"

"She says she'll call you when you're better. That she loves you, and is proud of you, whatever that means," Ruth passed along. "And you need fluids, and to use bleach spray on anything we've touched."

"Of course. Priority, germ eradication." As soon as he could summon the energy to stumble to the kitchen, he'd get right on that.

Chapter Eleven

Maggie showed up on Asher's doorstep about twenty minutes after they hung up, with all the supplies necessary to clean away flu funk. She couldn't say that playing nursemaid was a role she'd expected to take on this early in a relationship, but it felt surprisingly comfortable.

She'd been worrying about Ruth's health for days, and when she'd heard Asher sounding like he'd been run over by a truck, all she'd wanted to do was make it better. She'd provide as much comfort as she could, and would sanitize the heck out of his house—that part came with the veterinarian job description. Yeah, she had a cleaning staff at her clinic, but back when she'd been a teenager and her grand-father was the animal doctor, she'd earned her time with the animals by mopping floors and disinfecting instruments. And if Asher had been up all night, he wouldn't be up for scrubbing toilets and faucets.

She knocked on the door, ever aware that Jackson might react to a doorbell.

Ruth answered, sporting a Wonder Woman nightie and some major bedhead. She looked none the worse for wear after her own bout with sickness.

"You have your color back," Maggie said, chest filling with relief. The urge to wrap Ruth in a hug came over, but she wouldn't push. "Which means that after we do a little maintenance work, we can hit the town. As long as it's okay with your dad."

"He's sleeping." Ruth stepped to the side, eyeing the bucket. "We have cleaning stuff, you know."

Maggie smiled and made her way into the ground floor hallway, which ran down to what looked like a laundry room and the entrance to the garage. Stairs climbed to the living space. She toed out of her lace-less sneakers, leaving them next to a shelf filled with Asher's funky collection of brogues and boots, and Ruth's sparkly sneakers.

"I figured you'd have something," Maggie said. "But this way, I knew what I was working with."

Ruth's face was a little thundercloud. "I told my dad I could clean and that I'd make him soup."

Maggie's throat tightened. Crud, she did not like

that frown. "That all sounds great. You can for sure do that. But like my grandmother said, many hands make light work."

"My grandma says that, too," Ruth grumbled. She stomped up the stairs, disappearing into the gap at the top. Jackson sat on the landing, head turning between Maggie and his new, pint-size master.

"Go on, buddy. Go to Ruth."

Maybe if Maggie couldn't soothe Ruth, the dog could.

He ahrooed at the command before tearing after the girl, a gangly mass of long limbs. The footsteps of both dog and girl sounded on the second staircase overhead, to what had to be a third floor, probably where the bedrooms were.

Maggie took a breath, contemplating the lack of welcome from Ruth. The kid was less than impressed about her impromptu babysitter. Maggie would have to sweeten the pot somehow. Crumb cake. She'd really hoped Ruth would be more receptive now that she was feeling better. What if she never accepted Maggie? The thought of not being with Asher because Ruth wasn't ready... She didn't even want to go there. She headed for the second level. When she reached the landing, Ruth was nowhere to be seen. She pressed her lips together and tried to breathe away the fear piling in her chest—what could she do to put Ruth at ease?

Leaving her bucket on the floor, she looked

around. A living area graced the left of the long, narrow space. A rustic dining set provided a transition in the middle, and the kitchen wrapped around the right end, centered by a granite-topped island. The place was decorated in a spare, mismatched way. Cute, though. Homey touches in the artwork and the collection of guitars on stands in the corner. Some pillows and blankets on the couch, most of which was taken up by a built, exceedingly male body.

Oof. His olive skin tone had paled to a greenish gray. Some of that soup Ruth mentioned might do him some good, if he could stomach it. Probably needed the rest more, though.

With him looking so darn ill, it made it easier to ignore the muscles of his legs, only covered by plaid boxers, and how his well-worn T-shirt molded to his pecs.

Easier. Not *easy*.

Resisting the desire to go to sit with his head in her lap in a vain attempt to soothe his misery, she pulled a velour blanket over his legs and went to work on cleaning the kitchen. She couldn't do anything to speed up his recovery, but she could at least make sure he didn't have a ton of house maintenance to catch up on. And once Ruth had warmed up to the idea of having Maggie around for the day, Maggie could entertain her, too.

If she warms up at all.

Ruth thumped down the stairs right as Maggie

was wiping down the counter in the powder room off the living area. The girl had changed into a sweater, skirt and tights. Her hair was combed down around her face, and she held out an elastic and a brush. "Can you do unicorn tails?"

Maggie froze. "Uh, unicorn tails?"

Ruth sighed. "That's what Dad calls ponytails."

"Yeah, sure." She hadn't styled much straight hair in her life, but it couldn't be that challenging. She took the brush and elastic and stood at Ruth's back, gathering and smoothing the long, dark strands. She laughed as she kept losing her grip. "Your hair is so much slipperier than mine."

"I wish I had curly hair," Ruth lamented. "Mine doesn't look like my dad's or bio mom's at all."

"It's lovely. And being so long, I bet there are all sorts of YouTube tutorials for braids and stuff that wouldn't work with curly hair."

Ruth paused, expression hopeful. "Would you do one for me?"

A thrill of victory ran through Maggie. Hair-dos weren't something you shared with just anyone. Maybe she was making some progress, after all. "Yeah, sure. We can find one on my phone."

They spent a few minutes searching for a style that piqued Ruth's interest, and then relocated to the kitchen table for the actual styling. It meant being quiet so as not to wake Asher, but that was okay. Maggie would rather Ruth not feel like she had to make conversation. It was better to have it come naturally.

After Maggie wrestled Ruth's hair into a passable interpretation of the half-up braid-and-twist combo, the girl ran upstairs to inspect it in the mirror. Maggie followed, bringing her bucket and spray with her. Asher's bedroom was up here, and she was dying to take a peek. He'd seen how she decorated her personal domain, after all. But would he want her in his space? She'd start with the main bathroom, and get a read off Ruth as to how private he'd be.

"More cleaning?" Ruth asked warily, watching Maggie arm herself with gloves and disinfectant. Jackson stood at the doorway, and flopped to the ground in the hall when Maggie signaled him with a hand.

She cleared a Princess Leia cup holding a purple toothbrush to the side. "All right, Ruth." She handed over extra gloves and a rag. "Has your dad ever conscripted you for disinfectant duty?"

Ruth put the gloves on. They looked comical, stretching up to her elbows, plastic sausage fingers clutching the cloth Maggie had rooted out of a cupboard. But her pulled-together brows were the opposite of humorous. "My *dads*."

Maggie didn't want to read the inflection the wrong way. But she also didn't want Ruth to think she wasn't fully aware of Asher's marriage, that she was willfully ignoring it or anything. "Yes. 'Dads.'

That's important. You call Asher 'Dad'—remind me of your name for Alex?"

Ruth's concern shifted to solemnity. "Papa."

"Cool. And what was he like? I mean, if you want to tell me about him. No pressure." Maggie started spraying door handles and the toilet, pretending to look casual so that Ruth would relax.

"He loved animals like you do." Ruth followed behind her, polishing the door handles with precise little swipes. "He always wanted a dog, but he and Dad decided one wouldn't fit in our apartment." Her lip wobbled. "I wish he could meet Jackson."

"Jackson's pretty special. And I bet your Papa was, too."

Ruth nodded. "Can I have the spray?"

Maggie handed it over, starting on the toilet while the girl decked the sink with disinfectant. "Did he have a favorite animal?"

"Cats. Maybe." Her face crumpled. "I don't know."

Way to go, Maggie, reminding the kid that her knowledge of her father is incomplete. Her heart clenched. Memory was so finite. And fragile. "That's okay. I'm sure your dad knows."

"Yeah, probably." Ruth sucked in a breath, making her nostrils flare. "I could ask. When he wakes up."

Which didn't happen for a while. She and Ruth managed to finish the cleaning, get into a serious analysis of Ruth's collection of dragon and unicorn figurines and even take Jackson for a walk, all while Asher sawed logs on the couch.

"So, what did you mean when you said we'd hit the town?" Ruth whispered, standing next to Maggie as they hovered in the kitchen.

"I thought we'd find lunch somewhere. And then we could try out the ski simulators at the health center."

Ruth's face lit up. "That would be awesome!" Asher stirred, and she slapped her hand over her mouth. "Sorry, Dad."

"S'okay," he grumbled.

"Asher, mind if I take Ruth for lunch and to the gym?" Maggie asked.

His eyes stayed shut and he covered his face with his palm. "Mmph, sure."

"We're on," Maggie said, holding her hand up for a high five.

Ruth jumped up and slapped palms.

Maggie smiled to herself. Maybe she knew what she was doing after all.

An hour later, Ruth was grinning wide enough to boost Maggie's confidence all the more.

"This is so much fun!" Ruth gripped the arched bar on the front of the ski training machine with both hands. Her feet were encased in ski boots, attached to the bindings of the simulator. She swooshed from side to side, mimicking the motion of downhill turns. The hairstyle Maggie had worked to perfect was starting to fall from the elastics.

"You've really got the hang of it," Maggie called over from her own machine. Sweat dotted her forehead. Yikes, this was a good workout. "You're gonna be dynamite on actual skis."

"I so am!" Ruth exclaimed, grinning wide enough to compete with the overhead lighting of the gym's ski-training room. Six machines populated the space, as well as free weights and other equipment.

Maggie chuckled and turned to Garnet, who stood next to Maggie's machine. "Thanks for arranging this."

Garnet operated her part-time acupressure business out of Evolve Wellness and had arranged for Ruth and Maggie to use the training area. She'd snagged a pair of boots in Ruth's size from the mountain's rental shop, too. "Of course. She's going to officially be my niece soon." Garnet lowered her voice. "And maybe something more for you."

Maggie's heart lurched into her throat. *"Garnet."*

Her friend regarded her, freckled face all innocent and in complete opposition to her pot-stirring. "What?"

"I don't know what's happening with—"

"Of course you don't." Garnet shrugged and leaned against one of the other ski simulators. Given she was on the premises to see clients in an hour, not to work out, she wore leggings and a long, turquoise T-shirt. Her red curls were pinned up in a complicated yet messy style. "No one knows anything, Maggie. There are no guarantees."

Maggie paused in swinging from side to side. "Are you and Emma in cahoots or something?"

Garnet shook her head. "No, I'm saying that I've had my own rigid thinking about love and relationships. And when I met Caleb, I learned that keeping an open mind is a good thing. The frameworks we create to protect ourselves can be important through certain stages in our lives, but sometimes we outgrow them."

"Is it even possible to outgrow bad parenting?" Maggie blurted. Ruth perked up and looked in Maggie's direction. *Oops.* This was not a conversation to have around ten-year-old ears. Maggie raised an eyebrow and tilted her head, silently trying to get that across to Garnet.

Garnet nodded her understanding. "We're not done with this, though."

"Oh, really? Since when are you the emperor of relationships?"

"Since I fell in love with a Matsuda," Garnet whispered. "I highly recommend it."

"Hey, sleeping beauty." Asher heard Maggie's voice filter through his dozy state. Something cold swabbed his forehead—a cloth?

And then there was warmth against his cheek. Her palm. He let his head loll into her cupped fingers.

"You shouldn't touch me," he warned. "You don't want to catch this."

"I'll wash my hands. Plus, I sanitized your kitchen and bathrooms."

"You were talking to my mom, weren't you?"

"No, to Ruth, who passed on the message from your mother. I showed her all sorts of things about de-germing. And then we took Jackson for a walk. And she seemed to really like the ski simulator."

He opened his eyes, soaked in the sight of Maggie kneeling on the floor beside the couch. Hair pinned up in segments, tight at the front and a halo in back. The rich brown of her eyes caught the sun from the living room window. He blinked at the brightness. If the sun was coming in at this angle, he'd been sleeping for... Three hours? Four? "Holy crap, Maggie, I'm so sorry. You didn't need to step in like that. I could have woken up and done my dad duties."

"Asher Matsuda, if you so much as move from this couch today, other than to use the washroom, I will actually call your mom and rat you out."

"You wouldn't."

She laughed. "No, but I bet Ruth would."

"Truth." He groaned.

"Ruth ate, in case you were wondering. I grabbed her a grilled cheese for lunch, and she finished most of it, but she was feeling pretty bagged once she was done at the gym. I hope I didn't wear her out too badly."

"If she was willing to go, it meant she had the energy. I, meanwhile, can barely make it off the couch."

"You are looking a little rough. Pretty as always, but ailing." She brushed his hair back from his face. With a gentle hand, she massaged his scalp, pausing every once in a while to finger-comb a tangle.

"I lay down with wet hair," he explained. Now that he'd slept, he felt just human enough to want to look somewhat presentable.

"I figured you wouldn't be your usual natty self." She lifted a corner of her mouth. "You have a bad bug."

"Not surprising I caught it after holding Ruth's hair back for two days while she threw up. And like I said, you really shouldn't be here."

"Someone needs to be."

Alex. Grief pulsed in his chest, brief but strong. But a chuckle broke the sadness. For all that Alex had been a tenacious patient, he'd lacked nursing skills. Any time Ruth had been sick, Alex had let Asher take the lead. And when Asher had been the one down for the count, fat chance of getting a cold compress.

Maggie cocked her head and paused her massage. "Something funny?"

"Yeah, how much Alex hated being around sick people. He forced it for Ruth's sake, occasionally for mine, but his bedside manner was not his strong suit."

She stared at Asher, eyes full of questions.

"What's putting that look on your face? You can say it," he said.

After a long breath, she said, "Must have made it extra hard for him to *be* the sick person."

"Surprisingly, I think it was the opposite. He hated seeing his loved ones suffer. Found it much easier to be the one in the tough position."

"You were all in a tough position," she whispered.

"We were," he agreed. A pang of longing struck him. "This is one of those days I wish he was here. Even though he was a terrible nurse."

Maggie inhaled sharply, inching away from the couch. "Oh. I guess… Well, that makes sense."

His stomach twisted worse than it had when he was at his most nauseated in the middle of the night. "Damn, Maggie. That came out wrong."

Closing her eyes for a second, she took what looked like a centering breath. "Can you explain what you meant?"

"Yeah, of course. I miss having him to lean on. Knowing the intricate parts of life that kept a household running. Being able to chip in extra when he needed it, and having him do the same for me." He swallowed, the lump in his throat made of grief, and a whole lot of fear that he'd push this woman away. "But the fact I miss having that with him doesn't mean I can't find it with you."

"You're sure about that?" she asked carefully.

"I am."

"Okay." She crossed her arms. "I'll have to trust you, I guess."

"You can."

Maggie's lower lip tightened and she glanced to the side.

"Dad?" Ruth's voice came from down the hallway.

"Hey, peanut," he greeted. Her cheeks were back to a healthy pink. At least one of them was on the mend. "Thanks for letting me sleep."

"You were snoring. And we had a good time." She relayed their activities, a similar recounting to what Maggie had given him, but with a touch of ten-year-old hyperbole for flavor.

"I can't thank you enough, Maggie," he said, hugging one of the squishy throw pillows to his chest to keep from reaching for her. "I owe you. And I'm officially behind on the work I promised."

She shook her head. "Life happens. And I tell you what—as long as Ruth is up for it, she and I could go over to the addition and could move whatever tools and supplies are in the multipurpose area into the conference room. That way Lachlan can use the big room for his class tomorrow. As long as the floor's clean, he can live with the cabinets being unfinished."

"I'll owe you."

"Take me out for dinner when you're feeling better, and we'll call it even," she said with a wink.

Chapter Twelve

Maggie sat in her desk chair on Monday afternoon, swinging herself back and forth with the toe of her work sneaker. There had been so much to take in yesterday, and she was struggling to make sense of it. That Asher still missed his husband—that wasn't a surprise. Of course he did. But the degree to which he wished to have Alex back?

Harder to process.

When he'd told her that, the realization had struck hard: Alex would always be a part of whatever relationship she had with Asher and Ruth. And trusting Asher's assurances that he was ready to build something with her didn't come easy. That *Ruth* was ready to make that change. Trusting someone romantically after growing up with no faith in love was hard enough. Parenting was another thing entirely...

At least I didn't bolt.

That was progress. She'd shocked herself when she'd resisted the urge to flee. It had been nearly impossible to stay put after Asher had announced he wanted Alex with him—how else could she take that to mean anything but that she didn't live up to his husband's example? But she'd forced herself to stay, to ask for clarification.

And he'd said all the right things.

Add that to yesterday having been great with Ruth—styling her hair, taking her to the ski simulator, the marathon string of Uno games they'd played in front of the space heater in Lachlan's office when they'd gone to the addition to move Asher's things from the main room.

It felt right, earning a place in Ruth's life. They needed a whole lot more time together, but Maggie was starting to wonder if she had the right instincts to be a mother figure, despite having grown up with the opposite.

But wondering was too wishy-washy. Taking that final step with both of them—believing she could be a mother to Ruth and laying her heart in Asher's hands—didn't come so easily.

Snatching her cell off her desk, she shot off a rapid text to a joint thread she had with Garnet and Emma.

How do I let myself fall in love?

Wow, that looked ridiculous in a text bubble. Her friends must have thought so, too, because they didn't respond. Possible they were at work. Or they were on a separate text thread, hashing out what they should say before they responded.

She killed time for a few more minutes. She both wanted advice and was petrified of having to take it. When her phone buzzed twice in rapid succession, she almost hit the ceiling.

Emma: Just be honest about what you're feeling, Maggie. Talk to him.

Garnet: Emma's right.

Oh for crying out loud, they *were* colluding against her.

See you at the barn in an hour?

That one wasn't from Emma or Garnet.
Asher.
Maggie cracked a smile. Her chest warmed.
Be honest... Talk to him...
See you in the barn.
Put it together, and she had her answer.
She wiped her sweaty palms on her scrub pants.

Talking to him in the barn in an hour. Sounded easy, but was pretty much the hardest thing.

Before she could muster the courage to head home and change, Lachlan poked his head in her office.

"Take off, Maggie," he said. "Marisol's ducking the weather over at Zach's with the baby, so I'll stick around to touch base with Asher. He figures he should be done by the end of the week."

"I know," she said. "He was worried after being sick yesterday, though."

Bracing his hand on the doorjamb, Lachlan cocked a brow. "You talked to him?"

"I… I hung out with Ruth for a while, given he was under the weather."

Lachlan grinned. "Marisol told me."

Irritation flared up her neck. Why Lachlan had to commit to being the annoying youngest sibling so well, she didn't know. "So why did you ask? You are such a pain in the rear."

"Then I'm doing my job."

"Since when does anyone in our family ever do their job?"

The accusation hung in the air, dripping with decades of suppressed resentment.

Lachlan blinked in shock. "When have I *ever* not been there for you, Maggie?"

"That's not what I meant."

He crossed his arms. "Maybe not, but you said it, and I think it's true to a point. You're always waiting for the rug pull, aren't you? Even though Grams and Gramps showed you what a home could be, and I've had your back since we were kids. Why do you have to give Mom and Dad so much power over your life? You and Stella both—you're so damned afraid, and you're missing out."

If it had just been Garnet's reminder about growth yesterday, or Lachlan's rebuke today, Maggie might have been able to ignore them. But to have two people in her life deliver such similar messages...

She lowered her gaze and swore.

Lachlan slipped sideways against the door frame, barely catching himself before he toppled over. "What did you say?"

"Something that was right two seconds ago but doesn't need to be repeated," she said between gritted teeth.

"No, say it again," he encouraged. "Let it out, Maggie. Whatever you've been holding in that brain of yours—that heart, more likely—for so long."

"I don't need to swear again, Lach," she said softly. "But I could open up some. Especially with Asher." Her throat tightened, but she fought the fear. Asher was an amazing person, who had a whole lot on the line himself. He'd listen and would support her, no matter what it meant for them going forward. It would just take being fully honest about where she was coming from and why she was so stinking afraid. Afraid she wasn't good enough and would never live up to Alex's memory. And maybe with admitting how she felt, she could lose some of that fear. Enough to create a future with him and Ruth.

An hour later, Maggie waited in the main area of the barn, but stacking and restacking various supplies could only keep a person busy to a point. Nerves skittered along her skin as she tried to put her thoughts in logical order. She'd sent her brother home after their chat and had stuck around to finish paperwork. She glanced down at her purple scrubs and utilitarian sneakers. Why had she not run home to get changed? Asher would be here any minute, and her work clothes weren't exactly the height of fashion.

She was in the middle of reorganizing a training supply cupboard when Ruth and Jackson tumbled into the main area of the addition, a tangle of blue-gray dog limbs and messy pigtails.

"Can I read my book on the couch in the office?" Ruth asked. "I'm almost done this awesome story about dragons. Except they're cats. And there's a portal. It's so cool."

"That does sound cool," Maggie said. "And help yourself to the couch. The heater's there if you get chilly."

Asher strolled through the front door as Ruth tore down the back hallway, Jackson loping at her heels.

His gaze went smoky as he looked Maggie up and down.

Son of a biscuit, that slow grin... It lit a fire in her belly.

But they'd have to wait to explore that. They had far too much company and needed to talk.

He closed the space between them and brushed his fingers along her cheek. "Have I ever told you how cute you look in scrubs?"

Her heart hammered, and she took the easy route—going for casual banter rather than asking him to come to her office so she could spill her guts. "Just what a grown woman wants to be—cute," she said, pretending annoyance.

He peeked behind her, appearing to check for his daughter's presence. With a satisfied half smile, he dipped his lips to forehead. "I'd kiss you, but I want to make sure I'm not sick anymore."

"A hug's good, too."

Getting to see this man was really the perfect way to end her workday.

Work up some courage, and you might be able to come home to him, too.

He drew back. "A person can be more than one thing, Maggie. In your case, looks-wise? Sexy, beautiful, attractive—pick a synonym, any synonym." He smirked. "And I stand by *cute*."

She couldn't get past the first part of his claim. "More than one thing," she repeated.

Her grandmother had believed bad things came in threes. Well, advice came in threes too, apparently.

Asher shot her a puzzled look. "Well, yeah. We all have facets, Maggie. And I gotta say, yours fascinate me. Even though you're still keeping some of them from view."

She inhaled deeply. "About that... Do you think Ruth will be occupied for a bit if we have a talk?"

His brows drew together. "She won't even notice. The kid loves herself some dragons."

"And cats, apparently."

Maybe one day Asher and Ruth would want to move into Maggie's place and they could adopt a whole menagerie, minus the dragon—

Slamming the brakes on that fantasy, she took a deep breath.

"What do you want to talk about, love?"

How I fall for you a little more every time you call me that.

"I have so much baggage. It seems unfair to saddle you with it," she blurted.

He held up a hand. "You have baggage? I come with a kid. And grief."

She wrung her hands. "Sure, but even with the complications, you still manage to be brave. And I'm...not. I mean, sure, I had fun with Ruth yesterday. And I was glad to be able to pitch in and make your day a little easier. But is that really what a relationship is?"

"Well, yeah. Sort of." He studied her. "I mean, it's also sharing a glass of wine on a Thursday evening, and holding hands while taking the dog out for a walk, and sneaking kisses and a whole lot of mindless pleasure. But it's nothing exceptional. Your average relationship is exceptional in its normalcy."

"I didn't see a lot of normal," she admitted. "I saw Mom drinking wine until she passed out on a Thursday, and was yelled at when I dared ask for a dog. And mindless pleasure? Maybe my dad had that—with his mistress du jour."

He hissed out a breath. "God, Maggie."

She shrugged.

"But you've seen love, though. Your grandparents, your brother and Marisol. Hell, my brother and Garnet, too. I get your parents were a rotten example, and that leaves an imprint. Alex's parents' rejection hurt until the day he died. But the love in his life from his chosen family—me, Ruth, my family, our friends—it overflowed."

"It's so hard to trust that if I reach out, my heart will be safe. It's not just my parents. My ex-boyfriend left me and *stole* our *dog*, Asher—" Her throat tightened, making his name sound like a croak. "I didn't get to say goodbye. It's not the same as losing a person, I know. And I logically know you wouldn't do anything like that. But it's hard to break out of the mindset of that being what a relationship is."

"I—" He sighed. "Being vulnerable is risky. I

know that. I know exactly what it's like to fall, to commit, to love with my whole self and then when it falls apart to not be whole for a while. But I'm working at putting myself back together. I won't be exactly the same again, and I'm okay with that. And when I think about where I want to be, who I want to be with? I see being with you. And I hate the idea of taking the risk with you and not having it work out, or God forbid, losing you. But I hate the idea of not having you in my life more."

Her eyes stung. "I want you in my life, too. And Ruth. And I wish I was as resilient as you."

"It's a choice, Maggie. Before Alex died, he and I talked about me finding love again. He wanted that for me. I wanted that for me. But that didn't make it easy. I had to decide to actually do the thing. Hell, I make that decision every day. But I promised I'd move forward when I was ready. And with you—I'm ready."

"I—" She wrapped her arms around herself.

"Hey." In the absence of furniture, he sat with his back braced against one of the cabinets he'd built. He motioned her over. "Don't close up. Just this once. Come snuggle for a second, stay open with me. Push a little farther, see how it goes."

Farther. Stay open. Her heart pounded, but just like she'd tried extra yesterday and she'd managed to bond with Ruth, maybe she could progress here, too. She sat between his splayed legs, her knees bent over one of his thighs. She settled against his flannel-covered chest. So much strength, and not just physical. Yeah, he had muscle definition to spare, and his arms ringed her in a hug more comforting than anything she'd ever known. Enough to hold her and buoy her and make her feel like she might possibly be enough for this man.

And his daughter.

"I'm so afraid of failing Ruth like my mom and dad failed me. Teaching her how to work with a dog and braiding her hair does not a mother make."

"Uh, that's exactly what a mother does. Just like all those little things that make up a partnership? Same goes for parenting."

Hope pulsed at her center. If parenting truly was about the little things, then she could see herself being a mother, a mentor to Ruth. Would it really be that simple? She wanted it to be. So much. Except how could anything be simple? "There will always be a third parent in the room. A third partner. Someone you'll always deeply love. And living up to the example he set? Filling the hole he left in your lives, being the parent he was? I don't know if I can do that."

A gasp sounded from around the corner and Ruth appeared in the hallway. She dropped her backpack on the floor and hugged herself tightly. "No one can be like Papa."

Maggie jerked to sitting and tried to scramble out

of Asher's arms. He didn't stop her from standing, but he rose with her, keeping a hand on her shoulder.

"No one needs to be, Ruth. We all have our strengths and weaknesses." He lowered his voice and murmured, "Alex included."

For Maggie's benefit only, she assumed.

"Papa told me it would be okay if Dad found someone else to love. So why can't you love us back?"

"Oh, Ruth, I'm just…" *Scared.* Asher's hand tightened on her shoulder, and she took a deep breath. "Figuring things out."

"Peanut," Asher said, "eavesdropping can mean hearing things out of context. And hearing adults-only things."

"But you said you couldn't be a parent," Ruth cried, piercing Maggie with an accusatory look that cut her to her soul. "You don't like spending time with me?"

"That's not what Maggie said," Asher soothed, beckoning his daughter over with a hand.

She shook her head. "I don't want a hug."

Asher's posture crumbled a little.

And Maggie desperately wanted to hold them both up, knowing all the while she was the one pulling them down. Driving a wedge between father and daughter.

She couldn't let that happen. "I *love* spending time with you, but I want to make sure I fit in your life," she insisted. The truth burned in her chest like a supernova. She did love spending time with Ruth. Heck, she plain loved everything about Ruth. *And Asher.*

Reeling from that realization, she was slow on the uptake when Ruth whispered, "You don't want to be my stepmom."

"What?" Maggie said on a gasp. It was the opposite. She wanted nothing but that. Nothing but that and to be with Asher, obviously, but the two were part and parcel… "Ruth, no, I—"

"Ruthie," Asher warned. "You're getting carried away."

"No, I'm not!" She whirled around and ducked back into Lachlan's half-furnished office. The dog scooted in, almost getting his whiplike tail stuck in the door as Ruth slammed it.

The lock clicked.

Maggie's heart plummeted. "I messed things up."

Asher raked a hand through his hair. "Once she's cooled off, we can explain again, that we're not ready to think about terms like *stepmom.*"

"But I *was* starting to think—" *No. Stop. Listen to Asher.* So she'd had a realization she wanted to build a life with him and Ruth? That was no good, not if it didn't benefit them, too. And look at the rift she'd caused today—she couldn't guarantee she wouldn't mess things up again in the future. The prospect of causing problems between Ruth and Asher made her sick to her stomach. They deserved better than that.

Even if it meant letting them go.

Asher watched Maggie's face crumble. But it was more than her face. It looked like she was dissolving on the inside, too. Falling back into the self-protective patterns she'd learned while being raised by asshole parents, maybe?

Damn, he hoped not. *Okay. Think.*

He scrubbed his hands down his face. This could have gone better. But he and Maggie could fix it.

"Give me a sec," he said to Maggie before walking over to the office door and resting his forehead against it. "Ruth? Honey?" He pitched his voice loud enough for his daughter to hear. "Talk to me."

"I want to be alone!"

Maggie, eyes wide and hands clasped in a nervous knot, stood a few yards away at the end of the hallway. "I'll give you some privacy."

"Not necessary." Asher examined the lock on the door. It didn't have a safety feature where it could be opened from the outside with a bobby pin or anything. "This needs a key. Do you have one?"

She nodded. "They're over at my house—want me to go get them?"

"Uh, not yet. I'm going to see if I can get her to open the door."

"I'll head home so that you can try to talk to her

without me around. Text me if you need me to bring you the keys."

He reached a hand out to her, but she was too far to touch. "Stay, Maggie."

"Your daughter needs you."

"Which doesn't preclude you staying."

She looked unconvinced. "Yeah, I think it does."

He lowered his voice to make sure Ruth didn't catch what he said. "What are you saying?"

"That you should focus on your daughter."

Damn, the pain in her eyes. "I know I should, and I will, but look… I know Ruth. She wasn't bothered by you and me being together. She just needs to feel secure."

"I—" Tears shone in her eyes. "I want her to be secure more than anything. I wish I'd had that as a child—it's the most important thing. But if we stay together… I'll get between you somehow. And I can't let that happen."

His chest clenched. "How, Maggie?"

Her teeth tugged on her lower lip. "I already am. She locked herself in my brother's office."

"Kids have rough days," he murmured.

"You think I don't *know that*? That's exactly what I'm trying to minimize."

He mumbled a curse. "Maggie, I love you. And I'm pretty sure Ruth does, too. And I think you're capable of returning that. I really do. But you've got to believe it, too."

"I know." She stepped forward. Resting a hand on his cheek, she rose on her toes and kissed him softly. A heart-rending press of lips. "And that's what I'm trying to do. I want to believe I can do this."

"I'm good with trying. It eventually turns into doing."

Her throat bobbed. "But you deserve more than that, Asher. So does Ruth. I can't ever replace Alex, but until I can be sure I can be what you and Ruth need... This can't work." Tears trickled down her cheeks and she wiped them away with the back of her hand. "Coax your kid out of that office. She's more likely to come out if I'm not here."

"I wholly disagree." His chest burned—love, panic, annoyance. "But I'm fresh out of ways to show you that you're exactly what Ruth and I need."

"I'm sorry," she whispered.

"Don't be sorry. Just figure out what you need to figure out." He clenched his jaw. As much as he wanted to take the risk for her, it was something she had to do herself. And he and Ruth were helpless bystanders. "But you're right—until you do, I need to put Ruth first. Make sure she's not getting hurt. I'll call you if I need the keys."

Shoulders slumped, Maggie turned and headed for the door. Her footsteps receded. He hated that she was walking away. Hated that his daughter was hiding, too. He leaned against the office door again.

"Ruthie? What's the issue, here? Do you not like the idea of me dating Maggie?"

"She doesn't want me!"

They had a couple of layers of steel and insulated foam between them, but her heartbreak carried straight through.

Asher's heart squeezed. "She didn't say that, honey. She's being thoughtful about whether she wants to commit with me, yes. But Ruth—that's a good thing. It shows she wants what's best for both of us. It shows she loves us."

I hope.

A loud sniffle reached his ears. "What's wrong with me, Daddy?"

Oh, God, that was enough to crack his chest open. He held a hand to his rib cage, shocked he didn't find a bloody wound. "Nothing, Ruth. You're incredible."

"Why did we have to move? It's no fun being new and trying to make friends—" Her words broke off in a sob.

He flattened a palm on the door, his own eyes stinging. "Let me in, honey. We can talk it out some more. Figure out how to help you find your place."

"No! I want to be alone."

"Not happening. Maggie's gone to get the keys," he fudged. "And I want to give you a hug."

"I need to be by myself! Promise you won't come in."

"I can't do that, Ruth." His lungs shuddered with defeat. He could unlock the door and violate her need for space. Or he could sit out here and feel like the crappiest father in the world. Sliding to the ground, he leaned against the door, letting his head fall back on the cool surface. "I'll give you a half hour, okay?"

He heard her moving around, and the click of Great Dane nails on laminate.

"Ruth? You're good with a half hour?"

"Maybe."

"I'll be right here," he promised.

"And Maggie's coming back?"

"Like I said, getting the keys," he lied. Having his heart broken was one thing. But his daughter's was still too fragile to suffer another loss.

Chapter Thirteen

"What do you mean, you *left*?"

Ouch. That one singed the phone line between Emma's house and Maggie's for sure. Emma had spent the last five minutes riffing on that same theme.

And Maggie's eardrum was aching from the tirade. She'd explained what Ruth had said, and Emma was disagreeing entirely on how to interpret it.

Maggie flopped onto her couch. Not even a dog would fill the cavern forming in her belly. It wasn't her house that was empty—it was her heart. And it was entirely her fault. "Well, I—"

"What happened to talking to him like Garnet and I suggested?" Emma spat out.

"I did. We talked a lot. It was a disaster." An hour and a half later, and Maggie hadn't heard from him. He must have gotten Ruth to unlock the door from the inside and then locked up the building using the exterior key Lachlan had lent him. "And he obviously mended his rift with Ruth, so me leaving helped."

At least something good came out of that tire fire of an argument.

"What, exactly, did you tell her?" Emma probed.

"That I loved spending time with her."

Emma's snort burst through the phone. "Which you proved by taking off?"

"It's… It's better that way. If I'm not around, they won't get hurt." Her heart cracked. She'd get hurt. She already was hurting. Leaving stank.

"Sounds like the opposite to me, but what do I know?"

"You know a lot." Her friend might be single, but she knew loyalty. She'd grown up in a functional family. Knew how healthy parenting looked.

So maybe you should listen to Emma's gut instead of your own.

"I'm not going to tell you what to do," Emma said. "But you're not avoiding them getting hurt right now. You're avoiding *you* getting hurt. It's easier not to take the risk, so you're running. And that's crap, Maggie. That's not fair to them or you. You deserve to be happy. Don't walk away from Asher and Ruth. Trust that Jeff was an anomaly, and walk away from the pain your parents caused. Lachlan did. So can you."

A fist formed in Maggie's throat. "You say that as if it would be easy."

But when was easy ever worth it? It sure as heck wasn't right being alone in her empty house.

"Your childhood sucked, but your adulthood doesn't have to. You're caring and loving and generous. I'm tired of you being afraid," Emma said.

She swallowed, resisting the tension around her vocal cords. Emma was right. She wasn't trying to protect them. She was trying to protect herself. Which wasn't working. "I'm tired of it, too."

"So go do something about it."

She mentally peeled away the cold fingers gripping her throat. "I'm scared of screwing things up for Ruth like my parents did for me. But maybe I won't do that. When have they ever taken my feelings into consideration? I would never purposefully treat her like they did me."

"And you won't do it by accident, either. You're too aware." Emma cleared her throat. "You could call your parents, you know. If you need to start fresh. Tell them how they've impacted your life."

"I could." But what was the point? Talking to them wouldn't bring healing or closure. She wasn't going to change their behavior, nor would she believe them if they pretended to be sorry. But she could change her own patterns. She could finally believe that she deserved love beyond what they were capable of giving her. She needed to focus on the relationships she did have—Asher and Ruth, Lachlan and his family, Emma, Garnet and Caleb—rather than on the people who'd failed her by manipulating her or walking away. "I don't want to talk to them. But I do need to choose to act differently going forward. Find healing with the people I actually love."

And maybe Asher was still over at the barn working. She could apologize to him and Ruth in person. Thanking Emma and hanging up, she scrambled into ballet flats and a hoodie and dashed out into the sleet.

The kink in Asher's neck was legend. Happened when you fell asleep propped against a door. Crap. How long had he been asleep? Long enough for the dog to be whining and scratching at the door. And what the hell was smelling like burning plastic? His eyes watered.

Burning plastic.

"Ruth? What's going on in there?"

He glanced at the ceiling. A thin wisp of smoke escaped between the closed door and the jamb. Pulse skyrocketing, he got to his knees and pounded on the door with a fist. Goddamn it, why hadn't he gotten those keys from Maggie right away? "Ruth!"

A thin shriek layered over the whining dog. "Daddy!"

"You need to unlock the door," he yelled, trying

to keep his voice calm while he projected, but there was a damned fire in there with his kid and—

Head in the game, Ash. You got this. Alex's voice.

"Watch over our baby, sweetheart," he muttered, testing the door handle for heat—none, thank God— before frantically jiggling the lever. "Ruth! Where are you? Can you get to the door?"

She screamed, a petrified noise that had him two seconds from pissing himself.

The dog barked, and a steady stream of smoke leaked out over Asher's head. He yanked his phone from his pocket and pressed the emergency dial button. It was impossible to hold the phone to his ear properly. His hands were shaking hard enough to register on the Richter scale.

"Can you *get to the door*?" he shouted. "If you can, crawl as *fast as you can*!"

Another shriek, then a loud thunk as what he prayed was a ten-year-old body collided with the door. The handle jiggled from the other side.

"Nine-one-one, state your emergency. Police, fire, or ambulance."

"Fire! Sutter Creek Veterinary Clinic. My daughter's locked in an office," he said into the phone. "Ruth, you're going to need to unlock the door from your side, baby—"

The door opened with a click and a whoosh, and she and the dog barreled out in a billow of acrid smoke.

He coughed, then pushed Ruth and Jackson ahead of him in the direction of the front exit with one hand, still holding his phone to his ear. How was there an effing fire in a brand-new building? And why weren't the sprinklers coming on? "Keep your head low, Ruth," he said, ducking under the smoke and rushing out of the building behind his daughter and the dog.

"Sir?" the operator said. "Your daughter is locked in with the fire?"

"No," he said. The fresh air burned his lungs. "We got out. But the building's on fire."

"Asher!" Maggie tore around the side of the clinic, eyes wild with panic. "The office window—are those *flames*? Oh, my *God*, what happened? Are you okay?"

"We're fine, but yeah, something caught fire in the office somehow—Ruth got out in time, and Jackson seems okay." Reiterating the location to the 911 operator, he shuttled everyone farther from the barn. Icy rain spattered them, and they huddled under the branches of a towering pine tree beside the clinic, watching orange and white flicker in the window.

The window shattered, a sharp report. Flames licked out, climbing the edges of the frame.

Ruth whimpered and burrowed into Maggie's arms. Asher clutched them both to his chest, and even though his daughter smelled like smoke and his throat stung and Maggie and Lachlan's business was literally going up in flames, he had everything he needed.

Ruth coughed, then startled. She grabbed his arm. "Do you have my backpack?"

"No, honey. It was on the floor next to me in the hall." Oh, man. All of Alex's paraphernalia she'd collected was in that bag. No way could they retrieve it, though. Damn. "It's—it's gone. I'm so sorry. But what matters is that we got out—"

"Papa's letters," she shrieked, sagging against him. Tears smeared the hint of soot on her cheeks. "I need them!"

"We'll have to wait for the fire department," he said, squeezing her tighter. "We can't safely go back in."

Maggie broke out of his embrace, eyes wild with panic. "Do you have copies?"

He shook his head, regret burrowing deep in his core. "Stupidly, no."

"Was the hallway on fire?" She backed up a few steps.

"No," he said. "Just the office, but who knows how far it's spread."

She scanned the front of the building. "It's worth checking."

"No, it's *not*," he snapped. Ruth let out a sob, and he squeezed her tighter. "I know they're irreplaceable, honey, but no inanimate object is worth risking a life for."

She buried her face against him, shoulders shaking.

Lips set in a grim line, Maggie lifted her chin and took off toward the barn.

"Maggie!" he called, swearing a blue streak. The dog barked, and Asher grabbed him by the collar to stop him from bolting after Maggie. With Jackson straining in his grip on one side and holding up Ruth on the other, he almost lost his balance. Or maybe that was his leg muscles weakening from sheer terror as Maggie neared the barn. "What are you *doing*?"

"She can't lose her father again!" she shouted back, swinging open the front door and disappearing into the smoke.

Ruth screamed. The dog howled. Asher wanted to do both things, but Alex's reminder to keep his head in the game echoed in his mind.

"Think, think," he muttered to himself. Sirens sounded from down the street, but Asher could barely hear them from the roar of blood in his ears. Holy God. What was he supposed to do? He couldn't run in after Maggie. But he couldn't just stand here and watch her risk her life over a few sheets of paper, either. His heart threatened to explode from beating so hard.

"You did this," he whispered, wishing Alex could actually hear him. "Now fix it."

Ruth raised her chin, face a mask of guilt and horror. "I did this?"

"No, honey, I was talking to myself," he lied, his

voice cracking. Tears spilled hot on his cheeks. "It's my fault." He raised his voice as loud as he could. *"Maggie! It's not worth it. Come out!"*

"I love you, Daddy. And I love Maggie and she's in there and she's going to die like Papa—" Ruth collapsed against him again, an incomprehensible wail keening from her little body.

"She won't die, Ruth." He couldn't survive it, not again—

"Asher!" A commanding male voice came from behind him. "Get into the parking lot! You need to be farther from the building."

Keeping his grip on Ruth and the dog, he turned to face the person. Sheriff Rafferty jogged toward them, wearing street clothes and a grim expression. The fire truck pulled into the parking lot and the crew piled out and flew into action, stretching hoses and shouting orders.

"Maggie went back in," he said, gasping through tears. He jerked his head in the direction of the burning building. Burning... Goddamn it. "About a minute and a half ago. Through the front door."

Rafferty's face went ashen. "Inside?"

"Yes," Asher confirmed with a croak.

Swearing loudly, the sheriff jogged toward the barn. He seemed to check himself for a second before plowing ahead. One of the firefighters noticed, shouted at him to stop.

But he didn't.

And thirty seconds later, he emerged from the door, with Maggie in a firefighter's hold over his shoulder.

She was limp. Way too limp.

So were Asher's knees. He locked them to keep from falling over.

"Maggie!" he called. He muttered a desperate prayer, stumbling over the Hebrew that had come easily to him the last time he'd begged for the life of a person he loved.

Sheriff Rafferty jogged a safe distance from the building before shifting Maggie in his arms, stripping the backpack from her shoulder and laying her on the lawn.

Of course she'd gotten the backpack.

"Is sh-she o-ok-k-kay, Daddy?" Ruth shuddered in his arms.

"I don't know." He wanted to fall to the ground, but he couldn't. He had to stay standing for Ruth, and they both needed to stay out of the way while the first responders worked—

"She's breathing," the sheriff said, the relief in his voice a fraction of what flooded through Asher.

He hugged his daughter. "You know what, I *do* know. She *will* be okay." They all would. He'd make sure of it.

Why the heck was her back wet? And the world was so danged blurry. Something was dripping on her face, so Maggie kept her eyes closed. Her head throbbed, and her throat burned like she'd swallowed a hot coal. And almighty Cheetos, her hands felt like she'd touched a lit barbecue—oh, wait. The fire. Maggie coughed, gasping for breath.

Someone settled an oxygen mask around her face, and the cool stream of air forced its way into her lungs.

"Maggie Reid, you are a stupid woman."

The sharp voice came from her left. She knew that voice.

"No, Ryan, you're stupid. You deserted my sister." The mask muffled her words.

"Oh my God, Maggie." Someone knelt on the ground by her head. A big hand stroked her hair. Lips landed on her forehead. "*Stupid* is right."

"She is not stupid—she's brave!" a small, tear-rent voice insisted. "She got my *letters*."

Shoes—and paws, maybe?—scuffed the ground to her right. She cracked open one eye.

Ruth stood a couple feet away, gripping Jackson's collar in one hand and the singed backpack in the other. Asher's face, shattered with worry, swam in Maggie's vision. Had she ever seen anything so beautiful as this man and his daughter? She tried to smile at him, but the mask got in the way.

She went to take it off but a hand stopped her.

"Christ, keep your oxygen on," Ryan snapped. "I

thought you watched *This Is Us*. You don't run into a goddamn fire."

Not normally, no, but when a young girl was about to lose her most precious memory from her dead father, and all you could think about was how you would do anything to hear one *sentence* from your own father as loving as the thousands of sentences in that stack of letters? Then you did.

Because of love. She couldn't feel anything except love right now. For Asher and Ruth and the goofy dog straining to lick Maggie's face, and even her sister's jerk of an ex-boyfriend, who'd risked his life to chase her into a burning building because she had rejection issues and—

"Maggie. Breathe," Asher murmured calmly, his hand on her shoulder. "You're going to hyperventilate."

She locked gazes with him. His glasses did nothing to hide the tears clinging to his lashes.

"I love you," she said. She turned her head a little, facing Ruth. "And I love you, too, sweetheart. Promise."

A stretcher rolled up beside her. "Hey there, Dr. Reid. Let's get you off the ground and under a roof. You have a couple of burns that need attention."

Ah, that explained the barbecue hands. Crud.

"I saw her go down," Ryan said. "She was crawling on her knees. No C-spine issue. Burns on her palms and wrists, though."

Asher hissed in sympathy as she showed the EMT her wounds.

"That's a whole lot of ouch, Dr. Reid. Want me to treat you in your exam room, or do you figure we should head for the human hospital?" the EMT teased. He supported her as she sat up and shifted onto the lowered gurney, then promptly rolled her toward the parking lot. She lifted her head to keep Asher and Ruth in her sight.

"Stay with me, please." Even if her words sounded like she was speaking underwater because of the oxygen, she figured her pleading look got the message across.

Asher bent his head, handed Ruth his keys, and said something to her that Maggie couldn't hear over the noise of the firefighters and other emergency personnel. Ruth nodded and took Jackson out of view. To the car? Maggie's head swam as she tried to track the duo.

"Relax, Maggie. Put your head down and enjoy the comfy bed."

The EMT's dry suggestion made her chuckle, which made her hack and wheeze. He and his partner lifted her into the ambulance and started treating her burns.

A strong hand settled on her shoulder and Asher's face came into view. He settled on the bench opposite the stretcher and cupped both her cheeks. "Hey. I—I can't ride with you. I want to. Really. But I have

Ruth and the dog. And the EMTs want to check us out, too."

"It's okay," she rasped.

"No, it's not. I'll drop Jackson off at home and meet you at the hospital, okay?"

"It's just smoke inhalation."

"Maggie. You almost—" His voice cracked, and he took off his glasses and pressed the heels of his hands into his eyes. "You almost died. Don't pretend this is nothing."

"It's not nothing. You and me and Ruth—it's everything." She wanted to reach out to him, but the EMT was busy cleaning and dressing the hand nearest to Asher.

Fatigue creased the corners of his mouth. "Let's shelve that, okay?"

"I want to talk now," she croaked.

He looked up at the ceiling as if desperate for patience. "You sound like someone took sandpaper to your vocal cords." He sighed, and stroked her cheek with gentle fingers. "I'll see you at the hospital as soon as I can."

Chapter Fourteen

As soon as I can took way longer than Asher would have liked. An EMT from a second ambulance ruled out smoke inhalation issues for Asher and Ruth, but they weren't able to leave right away. The fire captain had all sorts of questions. Ruth clammed up, shaking her head whenever someone asked her if she knew what happened. Asher assured the captain they'd participate in any investigation. The drive to their town house seemed to take forever. Ruth was quiet in the back seat. Way too quiet.

"Ruthie, talk to me. I know that was stressful. And you need to be somewhere way more soothing than an emergency room. Do you want to go to Uncle

Caleb's house—Garnet's at home—or come to the ER with me? You might have to sit by yourself for a bit when I first see Maggie."

"I want to come with you. I want to see Maggie, too. But…but…" She sniffled. "The fire was my fault!"

He almost drove off the road. Catching the wheel before he yanked it past the point of no return, he slowed the car and pulled to the shoulder of the residential street. He turned in his seat to look at his daughter. "Say that again?"

"The fire was *my fault*." She buried her face in her hands.

His breathing picked up, and he worked to steady it. "How?"

"The—the heater."

"Like, the thermostat?"

She shook her head. "No, that black b-box heater that you had to dry the p-paint on the cupboards. Jackson was cold and Maggie said I could use it, so I p-plugged it in with the yellow cord and turned it on. And I fell asleep on the couch, and it was b-behind me, and I didn't n-notice it was on fire."

Oh, hell. He'd heard those things were notoriously flammable… "I fell asleep, too, honey."

How could he have done that when his daughter had been in such a state? Guilt razed his gut. He got out of the car and into the back seat and held Ruth for ten minutes while she cried over her trauma. Jackson, propped awkwardly beside them, stuck his nose in the middle of their hug and whined.

"Ruthie, you couldn't have known. It's okay. No one's going to blame you. I promise."

"What if Maggie's mad at me?"

"She won't be. She meant it when she said she loves you."

He'd gotten the impression she'd meant it when she said she loved *him*, too. He was counting on that truth.

After taking another minute or two to make sure Ruth was calm, he drove the rest of the way home where he secured the dog in his crate.

The five-minute drive to the hospital was excruciating. He jogged toward the hospital's emergency entrance, Ruth's hand tucked in his. Maggie had been alone for way too long, unless her brother had been notified—

"Hey! Matsuda!"

Asher jolted to a halt. Speak of the devil. He turned and waited for Lachlan to catch up with him. Ruth buried her face against his shirt, and he palmed the back of her head, supporting her.

"I hear my damned barn just burned down." The man put a hand on Asher's shoulder. "Thank God you all got out. You okay there, Ruth?"

Ruth shrugged, still hiding from the world.

Asher sent Lachlan a look. The other man nodded, seeming to get the message that Ruth was overwhelmed. Lachlan jerked his head and started off toward the emergency entrance again.

Asher hitched a step to catch up. "Did you come from the clinic?"

"No, I came from home. The sheriff called." They walked through the two sets of automatic doors. "I wanted to check on my sister first. Ream her out for running in after…what? A backpack, Rafferty tells me?"

Asher swore under his breath. More like running after the childhood Maggie'd never had. "Something like that."

The emergency waiting area was a long, narrow room with plastic chairs and terrible-smelling coffee. A nurse looked up from her desk as they entered.

"Maggie's in three, Lachlan," the nurse said. "Dr. Matsuda's in with her. You can go in as soon as he gives the all clear." She studied Asher carefully. "Dr. Matsuda's your brother, right?"

"Yeah," he answered. And thank God Caleb was on shift. Damn, Asher needed a hug. With Maggie in no shape to be his support system, his older brother would do just fine.

"How's Maggie?" Asher croaked.

"Just because you're related to the doctor doesn't mean I can give you patient information, hon," the nurse said sympathetically.

"What about me?" Lachlan asked.

The nurse sighed. "I'll say this—in serious smoke

inhalation or burn cases, protocol is to transport the patient to Bozeman. And as I'm sure you heard on your SAR scanner, Lachlan, no helicopters or ambulances have been dispatched. Now, sit tight for a few minutes, and you'll be able to go in."

"Thanks, Cath," Lachlan said.

Chest clenching, Asher dropped into a chair, pulling Ruth into his lap in an awkward embrace.

Lachlan sat down, too, leaving one chair empty between them. He gripped Asher's shoulder. "I'm glad it's quiet. I have a couple of questions."

"It's never actually quiet in the emergency ward," Asher muttered. How his brother managed his on-call shifts at the hospital, he didn't know. He dug in his pocket and extracted some change. He pointed toward a set of vending machines out in the hallway. "Ruthie, how about you go get yourself a snack?"

"Okay." She shuffled off and stared at the choices with her usual careful thought.

Lachlan leaned in and whispered, "So it was seriously your kid's backpack?"

"Long story," Asher said, keeping his voice low, too. Nerves shivered up his spine. Ruth may not have knowingly caused the fire, but she'd still contributed to it. Admitting that to the man who'd been dealt a blow to his business plans sucked. "You're going to want to talk to whoever set up your sprinkler system—it didn't come on." He took a deep breath. "Ruth told me in the car ride over that the space heater malfunctioned—"

"You're kidding me." Maggie's brother collapsed against his chair, tanned face paling.

Asher shook his head. "Ruth said she plugged it in to an extension cord. I'm so damned sorry—"

"She didn't plug it in to the extension cord. It was already plugged in. Maggie and I had both used it." Lachlan groaned. "And the sprinklers not coming on—the plumber had been there earlier in the day but didn't finish the job. Left the water off." He let out a low curse. "This could have ended so, so much worse. Your kid or you, or if Ryan hadn't gotten to Maggie... Hell, even your dog."

It was Asher's turn to squeeze Lachlan's shoulder. "Let's just be thankful rather than go down any of the 'what could have happened' trails, yeah?"

"Yeah." Lachlan scrubbed his hands down his face before peering at Asher. "I'm assuming if my sister's running into burning buildings for mementos, she's in pretty deep with you."

Asher's heart skipped a beat. "I hope so."

"Freaking finally," Lachlan muttered. He clapped Asher on the back. "When we get the all clear, I'll wait out here. You go in first."

"Ruth's too shaken up to be alone, I think. She thinks she's responsible."

Ruth returned to Asher's side, holding a packaged

Rice Krispies square. She regarded Lachlan warily as she fiddled with the blue wrapper.

"Sweetheart—" Lachlan rested his elbows on his knees and fixed Ruth with a gentle, genuine smile "—this wasn't your fault, okay? It was mine."

Metal curtain rings zinged on a rod, and Caleb rushed out of the cubicle.

"Is Maggie—" Asher's throat closed over.

"She'll be okay," Caleb said, hurrying toward them. "And am I glad to see you."

"Uncle Caleb!" Ruth ran to her uncle, who gathered her in a tight squeeze.

Asher's brother's haggard expression matched the accumulated stress that had been building in Asher since he first smelled smoke. He joined his brother and daughter, leaning into the family hug.

"Mom's going to lose her mind," Caleb said quietly. "Dad, too."

"We're all fine. You're sure Maggie's okay? I need to talk to her," Asher said.

"She needs to rest—I want to observe her for a few more hours and get another lung X-ray before I spring her. But she's been asking for you. Ruth can stay with me if you want a couple minutes alone."

"I do." Asher glanced at Lachlan. "That okay?"

Lachlan held up his hands. "She's asking for you, man."

Asher cocked a brow. "I might be a while. I'm a

book nerd with a penchant for singing my feelings. Being concise isn't my forte."

Lachlan chuckled. "Take your time. Maggie's been waiting many a year for a guy who's worth her time. I'm not going to be the one to steal away her romantic moment."

Let's hope that's what this will be. Maggie had seemed super sincere when she'd said she loved him. And that was a huge step for her. Would she want to do anything about it? But his heart was still bruised from her walking out earlier tonight—he couldn't take it if she retreated again.

Maggie poked at the cannula in her nose with a bandaged hand and sighed. She was alone. *Dang it. This is what happens when you push everyone away. They eventually get the message.*

No. Asher had said he'd be here. She had to believe that. She was just about to press her call button to ask if someone could call her brother or Emma when a hand nudged the curtain aside.

Asher slipped into the cubicle. His tired gaze took in the cramped space, stalling on the oxygen tank and the vital signs monitor and settling on the dressings on her wounded hands. "Holy crap, Maggie."

He came over to the bed and perched on the edge. And somehow, despite the tubing and wires and bandages, he managed to hold her. She melted against him. His shirt was still a little damp from the sleet, and his hair stuck up as if he'd been standing in front of a wind turbine.

"Think you have any pull with Caleb? I want to go home," she said. Caleb had told her to whisper, but not being able to speak at normal volume had made her question come out like a toddler's whine.

"Hell no. You'll stay until he decides your lungs aren't going to fill with fluid."

She sighed. "It's not that bad."

He stiffened. "It isn't? Breathing is kinda necessary. And what about your hands?"

"They'll heal."

Releasing her, he eased into the chair next to the bed and rested his fingers on her forearm. "It wasn't worth those letters, you know."

Okay, so Maggie had been rash. But making sure Ruth didn't lose her connection to her dad? It was worth a whole lot. "You didn't have copies."

"Who cares?"

"I couldn't let her lose that part of Alex. He mattered too much."

He pressed his fingertips against his eyelids, pushing his glasses up to his forehead. "Maggie, the best parts of Alex *can't* be lost. They live on in Ruth."

The words landed with a blow. She would have reeled back had she not been reclined on the angled bed. She'd always been so focused on how her parents had affected her in a negative way, she forgot sometimes that positive traits could be passed on, too. Was it the same with her parents? Were there any parts of her that reflected them? Her dad's tenacity, maybe. And her mom's ability to keep a bunch of balls in the air at once…

"You know what we did almost lose, though?" Asher's voice teetered on menacingly low. His fingers tightened on her arm. *"You."*

"You didn't."

"You *passed out*. In a *fire*. Had the sheriff not gone in— The firefighters were a minute behind him. What if…?"

"I know," she whispered. Knowing she owed Ryan Rafferty her life sat crazy wrong. How was she supposed to dislike him when he'd done something so selfless? But more importantly—had he not, had the firefighters taken longer to get to her, would she have been burned worse? Or succumbed to oxygen deprivation?

Oof. Nothing like almost dying to remind a girl she didn't want to die. And that she really wanted to spend her life with the man sitting next to her with a sexy beard and a jaw clenched so hard he was probably close to chipping a tooth.

"How did you burn your hands?" he asked.

She went to put her right hand over his where it gripped her left arm, but she could only rest it there. Her fingers were immobilized. Frick. It wasn't going to be easy to work over the next while. And training the Lab puppy due to arrive soon—so much for that.

"A piece of scrap lumber fell in front of me as I was crawling out. I pushed it out of the way."

A garbled protest escaped his lips.

"I'm sorry," she said weakly.

"Yeah, well, so am I. You were reckless, and I can't even handle that. But you're hurt. And I feel awful for being pissed off. But I am. So damn angry."

She blinked in surprise. "You are? You don't seem it."

"I'm a hell of an actor when I'm in a hospital, Maggie. I had months of pretending I was calm when I was sick to my stomach about losing the love of my life. And now I found you, and was starting to think I might just be lucky enough to have a second chance, and this happens?" Digging his hands into his hair, he flopped against the back of his chair and swore. "I can't lose someone else."

Her throat threatened to close over. From fear instead of the smoke inhalation, not that it was a better option. She sucked in a breath. "Right. I—of course. That makes sense."

He narrowed his eyes. "What makes sense?"

She loved this man so much. And she'd managed to remind him of the terrible price of love, and now he wasn't going to want to risk it. Right when she'd figured out her feelings, and that she was ready to take the leap. "That you wouldn't want to be with me."

"When did I say that?" Disbelief warred with the exhaustion lining his mouth.

"You didn't need to. I screwed up. This afternoon, with leaving, and then with the fire… I get it."

"Oh, love. You don't."

Hope leaped in her soul. "You're okay with this?"

"With you running into a fire? God, no. But with loving you? Obviously. Affection isn't a balance sheet. Not in a healthy relationship anyway. We'll make mistakes, miscommunicate. You'll even risk your life, apparently, though I could do without that one again."

She chuckled, wincing as the sound strained her tender throat. Talk about feeling like the worst case of strep ever. "First and last time I pretend to be the fire department. Promise."

Ah, crud, her search and rescue buddies were going to give her no end of grief for this. Rule one was never undergo a rescue unless it was safe for the rescuer.

She watched him scan her bandages and tubes, trying to figure out how to get close. In the end, he pulled his chair as near to the bed as he could and rested one hand on her abdomen and one on her elbow. "Your brother's in the waiting area. He's taking it pretty well, but still…"

"Oh dear." She shut her eyes, concern trickling into her belly. She'd been so worried about Ruth's letters and Asher's reaction, not to mention getting hauled out of a blazing building by her sister's ex-boyfriend, that she hadn't had time to process the impact on Lachlan's business. "Do they know what happened?"

Asher scrunched up his face in sympathy and gave her a short explanation involving the plumber, a space heater and an unnecessarily contrite ten-year-old. "A comedy of errors. Except it's not funny at all."

"We have insurance," she assured him. Her voice weakened with each word. She really should stop talking, but too much needed to be said. To him and Ruth. And thanking her brother and friends for de-livering her a well-deserved kick in the rear earlier today, making her realize it was time to move be-yond her past and find love with people who actu-ally loved her back.

Had she figured out her crap earlier, they might have avoided a near tragedy.

Her eyes stung. Her poor brother. Just because they had insurance didn't mean he wouldn't be bro-ken up about the fire. "We can fix the damage," she said, for her own sake as much as Asher's.

He rubbed a circle on her stomach and reached up with his other hand to stroke her cheek. "This is devastating, Maggie. There's no need to pretend otherwise."

"It's not pretending. It's…moving forward from something awful."

A smile flickered on his weary lips. "Maybe it's time to apply that to the rest of your life, too. You can't control how your parents or your ex-boyfriend treated you. But you can decide to live fully despite them."

Warmth—truth—flooded her bones. "Yeah, I can."

Happiness spread from his lips to encompass his whole face. "You won't regret it. Loving someone... Building a life with them... It's pretty damned awesome. Even with the painful parts."

She breathed in courage and nodded.

"You and your family are going to have to rebuild, and I want to be there with you through it," he said. "I just want the chance to love you. Will you let me?"

"It's not about the two of us, though. It's about the three of us. We need to have this conversation with Ruth, too. If we're going to commit, I want to hear from her that she's good with it."

He nodded and slipped out of the curtain, and a minute later Maggie's arms were full of tearful girl.

"Shh," she soothed, stroking Ruth's hair with the hand not hooked up to monitors and IVs. "Baby, shh. All's well."

"I'm sorry." Ruth's words were muffled against Maggie's neck.

"Me, too. I'm sorry I scared you and your dad, and I'm sorry I was too scared to be brave about loving you two. I... I was worried that if we got to the point where your dad and I were talking about forever, that I'd fail you. That I'd be a crappy mom.

You had a pretty great Papa, and I wanted to be sure I lived up to his example."

"You'd be the best mom," Ruth mumbled. She jerked to sitting, eyes wide. "I mean, if you want to. If you and Dad were talking about that. About forever and stuff."

Maggie smiled. Her eyes got wet again, but she didn't bother trying to wipe away the moisture. "I don't think we're quite ready for rings, yet. But you're okay with the idea that we might get there?"

Ruth nodded. She unclenched her fist and produced a folded sheet of loose leaf. She carefully flattened it. One side was a fill-in-the-blanks worksheet on the parts of a plant cell. The other was covered in slanted, blue script. The work of a man who'd been trying to record his thoughts during his lunch hour or preparatory time, no doubt.

Ruth held it out to Maggie.

Asher drew in a sharp breath and took the sheet. "Maggie's thumbs are out of commission for a couple days, peanut. I'll hold it. Where's the important part?"

Ruth pointed at the start of a sentence about halfway down the sheet.

Stay open to love. Don't let your pain stop you from enjoying all the minutes you're given. If you follow in my footsteps in one way, Ruthie, let it be that one.

"He said it to me, but if he was here, he'd say it to you, too," Ruth insisted.

A sob racked Maggie's chest. Oh, man. Having Ruth and Asher share their past and invite her into their future was too much to handle. But she was done questioning it. If they were willing to give it, then she was clearly worthy to receive it.

Ruth's eyes widened to stricken. "Are you okay?"

"Yeah," she rasped. "You're treating me like family. I'm not used to that. Or I told myself I wasn't anyway. Because my brother, of course, and Marisol and the baby, and Emma and Garnet and Caleb—" Her life was full. She already had a chosen family, and she wanted to add Asher and Ruth. It was time to focus on returning all that love rather than mourning the love she'd never get from her parents. Her future could be more than animals and lonely nights. It could be spending years and years laughing with and loving these two precious people.

She looked at Asher. His eyes were damp behind his glasses. Unable to touch his face or hands and connect in the way she craved, she smiled. "Family first, right? Can that—can it include me, too?"

He brushed her hair back and kissed her forehead. "It already does."

Epilogue

March wind nipped its cold teeth at Asher's face as he waited in the small spectator area at the bottom of the ski run. Maggie, bundled in a down-filled fuchsia parka, snuggled with her back to his front and held Jackson's loose lead. The dog wore a coat and neoprene booties and eyed the snow suspiciously, as he'd been doing since it started falling in November.

Asher stood with his arms ringed around Maggie—for warmth with the side bonus of getting to hold her. She gripped his forearms. Her mittens covered her scars, which had faded in the months since the fire. He couldn't tear his gaze off the small, turquoise-clad figure at the top of the run. "Good grief, I think I'm as nervous as she is."

And not just over Ruth's race.

"I know you are," Maggie agreed, turning her head briefly to smile up at him.

You don't know the full reason. Dipping his head, he kissed the skin right below the rim of her knit hat. The dog twisted around them, never letting them forget who had really brought them together.

Winter had flown by. A lot of time spent helping out the Reids as they rebuilt the barn. And he'd been so damned proud watching Ruth learning how to ski and fully catching the race bug. Caleb and Garnet had surprised them all with an impromptu January wedding, making Asher wish said wedding was *his* wedding... And every day was made better as he fell further in love with Maggie. He'd even managed to surprise her with a quick trip to see his parents and David a few weekends ago. They'd braved a New York cold snap—Ruth had toured Maggie around all their favorite Brooklyn haunts. Asher had strolled behind them, in his usual state of amazement as the daughter he adored and the woman he loved bonded and shared.

While there, he'd had a capital-*T* talk with his mom, followed by one with Ruth. And so long as Caleb showed up on time with the sign Ruth had made, he'd be having a capital-*T* talk with Maggie, too.

"Caleb and Garnet are supposed to be here by now," he grumbled, nerves panging.

"Ruth's up next—are they going to make it?" Maggie asked. "Did they text you or anything?"

He scanned the crowd, reluctant to take his eyes off his daughter from her place in the race lineup. He was about to scuttle his plan when he saw Caleb wending his way through the small crowd, holding a sign in one hand and towing Garnet along with the other. Asher waved an arm to get their attention before turning back to Ruth. She'd been living and breathing skiing since the mountain's season opener. No way was he missing a second of her first race.

Caleb and Garnet caught up to them in a flurry of Gore-Tex and woolen scarves. Garnet readjusted her floppy blue hat and clapped her gloved hands together. "We didn't miss her, did we?"

"You just made it." Asher motioned with an arm at the top of the run, where Ruth was lining up her skis and talking to one of her coaches. He put a gloved hand on the dog. Jackson had made enough progress with his anxiety that he was working successfully in Maggie's literacy program at the library, but still wasn't a fan of the crowd noise at ski races. They usually left him at home, but it only felt right he be present for the plan Asher and Ruth had cooked up.

"Sorry," Garnet said. "My morning sickness was heinous today."

His jaw dropped at the same time Maggie jolted to attention. They both stared at Garnet and Caleb, who were hand in hand, grins brighter than the sun reflecting off the snow.

"Uh, mazel tov," Asher said, blinking.

"Morning sickness? Are you kidding?" Maggie exclaimed.

"Nope," Garnet replied. "I would not kid about being sick as a dog. Oh, there goes Ruth! Forget I said anything."

"Crap!" Maggie whirled, and all attention was back on the dark brown pigtails streaking down the hill.

"Look at our girl go," Asher said, pride rushing through him. He'd congratulate his brother and sister-in-law with more exuberance as soon as his daughter was no longer careening down a mountain on two waxed planks of fiberglass.

Garnet cupped her hands around her mouth and jumped up and down, shouting encouragement. Asher joined in, yelling Ruth's name and ringing the cowbell that he'd bought special for the occasion. The dog leaned against Asher, and didn't jolt too badly.

Ruth skied like she'd been born to do it. Partway down the hill, she caught an edge, and Asher's heart almost stopped, but she recovered and regained her rhythm, finishing her last couple of turns. She crossed the finish line with a huge grin on her face. She took off her helmet and bounced on her skis, waving her arms in the air at her family.

Asher led the way to the area where the skiers

were corralled. His boots crunched on the hardpack, and he squeezed Maggie's hand. She was right by his side. Just where she should be.

"Dad! Maggie!" Ruth had removed her skis and was jumping up and down. "Look at my time! My personal best. Even though I caught my edge. That was my goal, and I did it."

He hugged her tight, wincing as the helmet and skis she was carrying thunked into his back. "You did, honey. I'm so proud of you. Way to work hard."

Everyone else congratulated her, and her smile grew that much wider. And when Maggie and Asher congratulated the parents-to-be again and Ruth deduced in seconds that she was getting a new cousin, Asher thought she'd float up to the clouds.

"Nice sign, Uncle Caleb," Ruth said slyly.

Caleb held it out to her, the Go, Ruth, Go colored in bright turquoise Sharpie to match her jacket. Garnet's doing, no doubt. "Want it for a keepsake?"

"I do." She shoved her skis and helmet into Asher's hands. Grabbing the sign from her uncle, she shot Asher a conspiratorial look. "But that's not what *I* would s—"

He held a finger to his lips and Ruth stopped talking. Maggie, who'd been squealing off to the side with Garnet about the pregnancy announcement, must have noticed the sudden shift in conversation, because she turned her head, expression curious.

"Go for it," Asher whispered to Ruth. He jammed

Ruth's skis in the snow, hung her helmet over one of the tips with a strap and dug in his pocket for his part of the surprise. Jackson sat obediently next to Ruth, as if he knew what was happening.

Nodding, Ruth opened up the false front of the sign to expose a new message. She held it under her chin and stared at Maggie with pleading eyes. "Will you?"

Maggie gasped. So did Garnet, Caleb and half the nearby crowd, for that matter.

Smiling softly at the shock in the brown eyes he wanted to wake up to for the rest of his life, Asher flicked open the ring box and got down on one knee in front of Maggie, his daughter at his side. "Will you marry me?" he said, in time with Ruth's, "Will you be my mom?"

Maggie dropped to her knees in front of him and took them both in her embrace. Mischief danced on her lips. "What took you so long to ask?"

* * * * *

Don't miss the previous titles in Laurel Greer's Sutter Creek, Montana miniseries:

From Exes to Expecting
A Father for Her Child
Holiday by Candlelight
Their Nine-Month Surprise

Available now from Harlequin Special Edition!

Get 4 FREE REWARDS!

We'll send you 2 FREE Books plus 2 FREE Mystery Gifts.

Harlequin Special Edition books relate to finding comfort and strength in the support of loved ones and enjoying the journey no matter what life throws your way.

FREE
Value Over
$20
